I0555456

PURE
SLUSH
BOOKS

PURE SLUSH VOL. 11

tall...ish

First published June 2016

Stories copyright © Pure Slush and individual authors
Edited by Matt Potter

Pure Slush Books
4 Warburton Street
Magill SA 5072
Australia

Email: edpureslush@live.com.au
Website: http://pureslush.webs.com
Visit the Pure Slush Store: http://pureslush.webs.com/store.htm

Original giraffe image copyright © Kym Parry
Cover design by Matt Potter

ISBN: 978-1-925101-80-5

Also available as an eBook
ISBN: 978-1-925101-98-0

A note on differences in punctuation and spelling

Pure Slush proudly features (both online and in print) writers from all over the English-speaking world. Some speak and write English as their first language, while for others, it's their second or third or even fourth language. Naturally, across all versions of English, there are differences in punctuation and spelling, and even in meaning. These differences are reflected in the work *Pure Slush* publishes, and it accounts for any differences in punctuation, spelling and meaning found within these pages.

for

Melanie

who

is

tall

A Tallish Tale
by Stephen V. Ramey

So there was this tall guy, and he had this Ziploc® bag filled with dirt. It wasn't actually full, but an empty portion is useless in a tale like this, so imagine it was full. He comes to the door – it was Sunday right after church – and he rings the bell and leans down and smiles for the peephole and straightens his tie, and eventually I do answer because… what else would I do on a sunny Sunday with a well-dressed man standing outside my door? I had a successful career, SUV, HBO, but I didn't have a man, and the sermon that morning had been on the emptiness of a life without a man, how Jesus lit up Mary Magdalene's life purpose by letting her wash his feet. Or something. I wasn't really listening. We had this report due at work and the data validation aspect was proving to be a bastard.

And this man, as the door opens, he says: "Good day to you, ma'am. How much will you give me for this primo soil?" So I'm thinking, Who buys dirt? I have a gardenful of dirt. I have a terrarium filled with dirt – well maybe not full, but full enough for the purpose of analogy.

I must have been staring, because the next I knew he had taken my hand. It was strong, his grip, and warm and kind and full, and I was kind of taken in by it.

"How much?" he said, and the bag lifted between me and the sun. Light shone through its pores. Light scattered a thought, how diamond is a type of dirt too, how everything is dirt in the end.

11

"I don't know," I said. "How much do you want?"

"That depends on how you value the things you encounter in life."

"I don't want to overpay," I said. A blush warmed my face. He chuckled, and I felt less embarrassed.

"What makes it worthwhile?" I said. "Does it come from a special place?"

"You mean like Grandmother's grave? Einstein's ashes? Harry Potter's potting soil?"

"I guess."

He lowered the bag. Our eyes met. His were serious brown with a touch of twinkle.

"If it helps," he said, "I put it on eBay yesterday."

"And?"

"It's priceless," he said. "Not a single offer."

"Oh." Was I disappointed?

"Look," he said. "Here's how importantly I view this transaction." And he peeled the plastic zipper. The opening puckered. I thought of his lips and how it might feel to kiss them.

He tilted the bag. "If you don't buy this soil, I'll spill it, let the wind and the world take it, and it will no longer belong to either of us."

"That doesn't seem... I mean..."

"Indeed," he said. "It would be a great loss." He tipped the bag until the first motes sprinkled down.

I stopped him. What kind of ending would it be, had I not?

He looked into me. I looked into him.

"Will you take a check?"

Slenderman's Tattoos
by Megan Crosbie

Slenderly, slenderly, I paint the last sign in tall letters: *Tulpa Tattoos – free today.*

I follow the signs back through the fog to my hut. I wait.

Eventually there's a stain in the grey haze. It wobbles closer, morphs into a customer.

I can taste his fear in the damp air between us. Still he comes in, lifts his sleeve. I crouch, fold my slender limbs around him to slip close to his skin, peach-fuzzy and still deliciously scented with youth.

I begin to drag the needle, perfectly scratchy, and oh so slenderly. The heat of his dribbling blood warms my fingers as I inscribe my mark: an 'x', trapped in an 'o', a nought and a cross. He will show his friends, and we can all play together.

Before he goes I clean his arm. I wipe the red and black smudges with my tongue in tender licks, oh so slowly and oh so slenderly.

The Two-Stall Bathroom in Nordstrom's Basement
by Samuel Cole

You want to know about my favorite public restroom,
    don't you?
Why I drive twenty-nine miles one way to get there.
How I shirk-work and race-pace and park-shark and so-lo.
Hint one: Lust and its Catch-and-Release Routine.

You want to know about my stall routine, don't you?
Why I sit on a toilet seat for an hour, often two.
How I wait-gait and play-sway and grow-show and
    ear-steer.
Hint two: Touch of the Here-and-Now Nirvana.

You want to know about the scent I crave, don't you?
Why I edge the partition to inhale male ripeness.
How I sniff-wiff and snap-trap and stretch-fetch and
    stroke-poke.
Hint three: Linkage to a Beg-And-Borrow Advertisement.

14

You want to know about my evolution of readiness,
      don't you?
Why I risk being caught for the few minutes of
      being caught.
How I knee-agree and hand-stand and feet-greet and
      finger-linger.
Hint four: Regularity of a Top-to-Bottom Lonesomeness.

You want to know about my tile-floor addiction, don't you?
Why I slide a prick and seed with willpower greed.
How I pitch-rich and bite-right and kiss-piss and strum-cum.
Hint five: Magnetism of the No-Strings-Attached Sex.

You want to know about my blowout letdown, don't you?
Why I ask for things no one gives or takes or shares
      or repairs.
How I lone-alone and blame-shame and stress-less and
      gait-late.
Hint six: Weariness of Restroom Anonymity.

You want to know about my afterward unwinding,
      don't you?
Why I curse traffic jams and the little children singing in
      car seats.
How I sigh-dry and door-floor and slink-drink and
      bed-tread.
Hint seven: Chagrin of Unsatisfying Repetition.

You want to know about my promise to not go again,
	don't you?
Why I make another round of inconsequential vows.
How I stay-away and snatch-latch and porn-scorn and
	blight-sight.
Hint eight: Deception of Seeker Changeability.

You want to know about my raging mind-fuck, don't you?
Why I fight an arcane root stymied by castigation.
How I frantic-antic and twist-list and file-nubile and
	haul-pall.
Hint nine: Pressure from Glandular Fixation to Recidivism.

You want to know about my self-acceptance, don't you?
Why I oughta be so ashamed you can't believe your eyes.
How I throw-glow and dim-rim and dearth-worth and
	my-oh-my.
Hint ten: Prince to the Outright Kingdom of a Beloved
	Pastime.

Joy in July
by Rita A. Simmonds

Red bird

bright

in dark green—

a mid-year reminder

of Christmas Eve.

The bird carols

volumes

from summer leaves—

Sing to me

sing to me

with your whole feathered frame—

the tallest tweet

to the smallest cave.

Building the World's Tallest Building
by William Doreski

We're building the world's tallest building
not in place but lying on its side
in a field west of Chicago.
Four two-thousand-foot steel tubes
form a box welded together
with a lacework of girders braced
by diagonals in a series

of four-hundred-foot X-marks.
Scaffolding holds it rigid
as we pour the thick concrete floors
and build ziggurats of fire stairs
and a sheaf of elevator shafts.
We rough in the wiring and plumbing,
then sheathe with bronze and glass panels.

We've built this massive skyscraper
without the loss of one worker's life,
no one subjected to altitude
greater than the mind can bear.
To install it we set rollers
down an avenue running straight
to the Loop, where a square foundation

gapes at the blue. One straight shot:
no turning corners with this load.
A hundred diesel tractors engage
the million-ton structure and drag it
past cheering crowds. Three days inching
to the site, where we line it up,
brace it at the lip of its base,

and lever it upright with jacks
with four-thousand-foot folding arms
constructed solely for this purpose.
The hiss of their hydraulic effort
muffles the usual traffic noises.
The skyscraper rises like a stalk
of sunflower, preening in the glare.

At last it's vertical and squared
and I climb a stairway to the top
and drop a plumb line. Perfect.
We bolt it to its foundation
with two thousand thigh-thick bolts,
hook up plumbing and power,
and install the elevator cars.

Ready to rent. We stand back and stare
up at our handiwork and watch it
breast the grainy wind off the plains
and feel every inch of it shudder
as the greatest Freudian pleasure
skewers us organ by organ,
bleeding us into the sky.

Wings
by Kristina England

I can almost reach the shut-off valve. If I were tall like my father, I would simply raise my hand and twist. Now, it's like I'm Stretch Armstrong or his feminine counterpart, created to be politically correct.

There is nothing equal in my inches. I can't grow to meet a man's mouth. I can't even open a jar, though I pump arm muscles for show. A couple more growing pains and I could have reached the knob. I strain on my tiptoes, but worry I'll pull a hamstring or worse, invoke my sciatica.

Instead, I grab a plastic storage bin because the stepladder is upstairs and I have been brought up on spoonfuls of laziness. I tell myself the bin can hold my weight. I am a woman, after all. We were made for light things.

I step onto it with my right foot, then the left joins without hesitation, without a moment's concern for the future. Perhaps this is how Icarus felt before he took flight. I don't have my father here to warn me about the sun's heat, but it doesn't matter. I too am as deaf as Icarus.

I reach for the valve again. This time, I don't have to overextend. As I touch metal, the world around me suddenly collapses. Shards of crate clip the basement wall. My legs plummet into concrete floor, the right pushing into contorted plastic. There is a moment where I see hell and it is hot white, not the red I believed.

I have fallen before. We all have. It is the human condition to forget our gravity and descend. We often sprout wings and they are useless. They are made from the wax and feather of hubris.

I see hell and it is only a flash. Somehow I escape the sea's dark tongue, her clog of bodies, and wake to my cat licking me.

I look at the stairs, ten to the top, ten to my phone. I look at my legs, large welts forming, the right in a horrid V. I turn myself onto my belly and crawl with the left knee, snaking my way up, step by step.

I am shorter than before. I am clinging to the wooden escapement as if it would devour the last slithering inches of me.

Somehow I make it to the phone. Somehow the length of the house does not swallow me whole. I shake off the wings and give them a dirty look because I know they will find their way back eventually. I will fly too close to the sun and plummet, perhaps harder.

I call my sister. She is the same height, but stronger. She thinks before she acts. If she was Icarus, if she was me, she could have survived the temptation of flight.

Tall Tree Tower
by Martin Christmas

Midway up the garden
between the flowering cactus
and the back fence,
and sometimes shading
the old park bench, and
sometimes not,
the itchy scratchy tree,
Norfolk Island Hibiscus,
the tallest tree
in the street.

We came here
after an extended holiday in the UK.
Mum fled there with we 3 kids,
not Dad. He stayed behind while
we went on an 18-month 'holiday'.
Made up. Back to Australia,
Adelaide. Planted
the itchy scratchy tree
from a seedling halfway up the back
behind this western suburbs'
late 1950s sandstone bungalow
that I have called home these past
eleven years, but in my heart,
not much longer.

Like us all, this massive tree
was once a seedling
planted in good faith,
and little did my parents know, I'm sure,
that it would grow and grow,
a magnificent tall tree tower,
though Dad's been dead 25 years,
and Mum gone these past 12
years. It is the tallest tree
in this, their street.

Grown from a seedling.

What will become of it
when I sell up
and move?

Pose
by Jolene McIlwain

His boots lay down a path through the Timothy and Queen Anne's lace. This tall, tall boy, with his long boy-legs, muscular basketball player's legs, strides through the meadow as warblers alight on stalks of ironweed, then lift again and call out.

The dog sniffs the bases of fleabane, goldenrod, bull thistle, then zigzags and looks back, making sure I'm following, making sure I'm still there. The dog knows the boy still needs me sometimes to lead the way, knows there are dips, crevices, brambles and briars, awful places to trip, snag, fall. He knows burrs will catch in his webbed Lab paws. He knows he could be swallowed by a groundhog's burrow pipe – a den of three or four holes. Still he dashes back and forth before the boy.

The birds are thrilled, chirping and trilling, seeing the boy ahead of me carving a path of his own.

I say "turn around," but this tall, tall boy of mine keeps his back to me, the hem of his T-shirt lifting with the wind. He knows the act of turning around to smile for the camera will lose this moment, will drag us away from the now.

Age Difference
by Alex Reece Abbott

Side by side, they troop along the baking pebbled footpath, almost lockstep.

Stride-stride-hop.

Hop-stride-stride.

Every weekday morning, Annie drops off Lee, then carries on two blocks up the main road to her school. Annie, in her crisp white shirt and red gingham skirt (hem measured to the approved length above the knee). Regulation Roman sandals, and snooty Panama. Lee, still in mufti.

The school run is an undignified scurry, a case of keep-up – Annie's legs are twice as long as hers. Lee doesn't grizzle, in case Annie leaves her behind.

She is with Annie and Annie is cool. Knows the latest fashions. Knows the Hit Parade by heart. All the pop stars. Every band member. Her blue textbook has a photo of a tower on the hard cover. (*Not the Eye-ful Tower, dummy!*). Some words are in English, and some are called French, this new code that Annie uses when she's showing off.

All their squabbles are ancient history to Lee now. The Chinese burns – even Annie's latest dastardly punishment, where she holds Lee's knees to her chest, then deposits her on the back lawn in the prickle weeds. Forgotten Saturday, when their mother only allowed Annie to see *The Sound of Music* with her best friend, Cushla, if they took Lee too. Always a reluctant babysitter, all day Annie treated her like a tag-along foundling.

Lee understands. She doesn't like having people foisted on her either.

Anyway, she knows their mother only wanted her there to spy and report back on Things. *Smoking; Boys; Other New Friends; Clothes; Boys; Parties; Unauthorised Purchases. And, Boys.*

Lee is calculating their ages in her head. Annie's haste makes Lee jerk, words spilling in a ragged, broken chant. "I am fi-ive ... so you're thirr-teen, annnnd when I'm thirt-tteen, you'll be ... whoah ... twenty-one-ah ... "

Without breaking her stride, Annie chips in, laughing at each new calculation.

It's no secret; Annie's in a rush. To get a job. Move out of home. Be a real adult.

Lee is torn between missing Annie and getting her own room.

Lee reaches *when I'm thirty-one, then you'll be ...* but Annie won't join in any more. They share an unspoken understanding, unable to see beyond that time.

Annie checks the time on her birthday wrist-watch. "Merde! Get a move on."

She grabs Lee by the wrist, propelling her so fast that her feet hover above the street like a cartoon roadrunner. A boy from Annie's class is dropping off his brother, so Annie's goodbye at the school gates is a casual nod and a tilt of her chin.

A noisy river of kids stream by. The asphalt driveway is already sticky, ballooning black bubble-gum. Lee watches leggy Annie marching off to Big School with Lanky Perry, until her sister is a speck in the shimmer, then gone.

They never talk about what happened when they played the age difference game.

When Lee finally remembers that day, she's the oldest, but still not the tallest.

Clock
by Melisa Quigley

From my four corners of the room
I am honest and truthful
My view is of the kitchen window
The sun casts a shadow of me on the opposite wall
Rain splatters over the window on a cold winter's day
And leaves turn from green to red and brown as they
    fall from the tree outside
In summer, children over the fence bob up and down
    as they play on a trampoline
Wrinkles adorn your face
My heart ticks away, but I do not grow old
I stay the same – stately and tall
My arms are shiny gold metal – long and slender
They point to gold numbers on my smooth face
I tell you what time it is every second of the day
You scowl at me when you are running late
Other times she scowls at me – impatient – wanting me
    to hurry up
I turn forward with grace and ignore you
You were once a young woman, now an old maid

A Present for Gandhi
by Martin Shaw

A Japanese silverback escaped to the jungle and decided to steal my leaves. I was chewing cud and dribbling down my beard at the time. He pummelled me senseless with the back of his hands, but not before I used his Yams to polish my horns. Doubled up in pain, he went from tallish to smallish as his screams echoed through the vines. Even Tarzan batted away the tweeting birds like butterflies to hear what was going on. Eventually, Jane beckoned him back to their love nest, craving more pork loin with apple sauce. Perhaps, if he was lucky, he could have a bit of Snarly-Benghali up the ol' jackdaw too.

Anyway, I awoke with a thumping headache and Old Mr. Silverback was doing the do-si-do, beating his chest to the world. *The show isn't over till the fat lady sings.* I scraped the ground with my hoof, using the fallen hogweed as a starter line to get a good run at him. Monkey Boy had his back to me, with legs wide apart in a John Wayne styley. Little did he know that sacrificing his yams to my Pagan skull meant no more emptying of nuts on wifey's birthday. I ran and jumped, butting his veterinarian's gastronomic delights, wearing them as a flat cap for a split second. There was quiet all around, except for the sound of heavy breathing, his nostrils expanding and contracting, while trying to take the pain. Suddenly, an enraged falsetto rang out across the pomegranates, bouncing from the tongues of my leafy cuisine. He did a stupid half run back to where he escaped from, holding his shlong. However, out the corner of my eye I saw something on my horns, smelling of a rubber plantation. I moved my head to make it swing, *like a pendulum do*, realising it was an empty sack – the torn-off scrotum of Mr. Banana Bukaki, the chimp from Nagasaki who wallows in mush of the yellow man's horn. Time for luxurious flip-flop making me thinks.

A List of Sideshow Performers circa 1885
by Nancy Stohlman

The Human Skeleton
The Armless Woman
The Elastic Man
The Human Torso
Jo-Jo, The Dogfaced Boy
The Siamese Twins
The Albino Family
The Giantess
The Snake Charmer
Boy With Breasts
Flip The Frog Boy
Stigmata Man
The Tattooed Man
Lobster Boy
The Strong Man
The Tall Man
The Four-Legged Woman
The Long-Haired Lady
The Electric Lady
Lion-Faced Boy
and
Hen Without a Bill

My First Beer
by James Wade

We used to shoot each other in the ass with paintballs on Fridays, until Bradley got adopted. Then it was just me and Martin, and it seemed dumb to shoot your friend without someone else there to laugh. Instead we hung around in front of the gas station – the one off Slate Rock Road – and asked people to buy us booze. I did the asking. Martin was short and didn't like to talk.

There was this one guy named O.B. – not Obie, but O.B. – who used to play baseball. He got paid a bunch of money when he was young, but he ended up getting kicked off the team because he couldn't pee into a cup or something. I heard Sharon tell the story once, but I wasn't paying attention.

Anyway, most people just ignored us when we asked for beer, but O.B. used to make a production out of it.

"Sorry little man," he'd say. "You gotta be this tall." Then he'd hold his hand about an inch above my head.

Every Friday for a whole summer I stared up at O.B.'s hand, always floating just past the top of my hair. And every Saturday morning I'd make Sharon measure me to see if I was any taller.

Even when I was sure I had grown enough to touch O.B.'s hand – he'd tilt his head like he was inspecting everything closely – he'd say no.

On the last Friday of summer it rained. I was wet and mad and had just seen Bradley eating pizza with his new family.

"Give me a beer, O.B.," I hollered at him as he walked up.

"Little man –" he started but I cut him off.

"I'm not little," I said. "I've grown almost two inches since school let out, so you better not put your hand anywhere near me, or I'll bite it."

Martin's eyes doubled in size and he started backing away, but O.B. just stood there.

"Two inches?" he asked, rubbing his chin. "Well, I guess I must've measured wrong."

He disappeared inside the store, and when he returned he handed me a red and white can.

My first swig of beer was not what I'd expected, but with O.B. eyeballing me, and Martin watching from over near the payphone, I wasn't about to make some stupid face.

"It gets better, the more you drink," O.B. said, as if he knew I didn't like it.

"Tastes fine to me," I replied casually, taking a big gulp.

O.B. smiled, set two more cans on the ground, and walked away.

I got good and drunk and made Martin promise not to tell.

The next morning my head was spinning and there was a nice-looking couple talking to Sharon about adoption.

"Too old… " they whispered as they walked past me, "… see how tall. But this one…"

They looked at little Martin and smiled.

I went out back and puked in a flower pot.

Measurements
by D.M. Simone

"How tall are you," Abby asks from behind Zora's desk, her face pale, her cheekbones sunken.

"5'10"," I answer through a yawn. My back hurts from leaning against the door frame of Zora's office. I secretly curse myself for offering Abby the chair I had been sitting in until her arrival.

"For real?" Abby blinks at me as if I had just come out to her as an alien.

That's how Fox Mulder must always feel like, I think and nod, then stretch my limbs to suppress another yawn. I ignore the once-over she is giving me, doubting my statement, remeasuring my height.

"*I'm* 5'10"," she insists.

"How big is 5'10"," Zora cuts in before I can reply with a shrug. After three weeks of staying with her I'm so tired of her ignorance.

"1.78m," I respond. "Approximately."

"Let's see if that is true." Abby struggles to stand up, then stumbles towards me and I wonder: is it really her boss who's the addict or her? "You're taller than me," Abby suddenly announces. Her feet are bare, mine elevated on a pair of flip-flops.

"Then add a quarter," I respond reluctantly, unwilling to continue a discussion I've been having all my life.

"178cm is 5'8''," Zora shakes her head, then presents the result to me on her half-broken smartphone with a smart-alecky smile.

I chuckle, "If she's 5'10'' and I'm 5'8'', someone must be getting it wrong."

"Tony showed me the app," Zora reinforces, her Eastern European accent stronger as she gets defensive. "He's a worker in constructing, he says me to take the app to get the inches right. It shows 5'8'', so it must be right."

"For twenty years I've been 5'10''," I moan before I can stop myself. There's no use in arguing with Zora, I should know better by now. "And now an app tells me I suddenly lost 2 inches?" I shake my head. "I don't think so."

"I'm supposed to be 5'10'', too," Abby remarks. She's crouched back onto her chair, a chair I really wish I had never given up for her.

"One inch equals 2.54 centimeters, one foot equals 12 inches," I sigh. "Just do the math."

"The app says 5'8''," Zora reassures Abby and I realize I'm fighting a losing battle. Six months after moving to the US, Zora doesn't have an inkling about the measurements, rules, history or customs of the country she claims to always have wanted to live in. I try to breathe but it is hard to catch my breath through my anger and pain. For twenty years I haven't been able to find a way to move to the country I feel most at home in, while her street smarts got her in without knowing any of the basics, while I know all the details. *Life's a bitch and then you die,* a Laura Roslin quote pops up in my mind. Fiction trumps reality, I laugh to myself then feel the urge to cry.

"You're 5'8''," Zora reaffirms, and I laugh out loud this time.

Tony's Wake
by Alan Walowitz

Anthony Peter Tumbarello (1945-1974)

His body, curled in life,
fit easy in the full-sized box.
A man wouldn't stand for one
cut for a kid and, God forbid,
made death seem airy and light.
I'd never been to a wake before
but you hear of the work morticians do.
Peeking in his casket
I half expected
the kiss of death
to turn the little toad he was,
my old pal, into a prince,
crowned and all aglow:
no longer a virgin,
lips puckered and set for a kiss
or at least to whistle a tune.
How about little Tony
finally straight and tall?
But, Death, even you,
in your high falutin' majesty,
you couldn't uncurl him after all.

The Giant, Snow White
by Liam Hogan

Yes, there were seven of us: seven *People*. Oh, and her, the giant, Snow White.

This story you *already* know: that's not what happened. It's not complimentary. That other tale, it's going to colour your imagination. Stories do that, good as well as bad. So sit back and listen carefully, but keep your interruptions to yourself, or I'll be up a stepladder so fast you'll never know what got your tongue.

You're trying to guess my name, aren't you? Even though we didn't bloody well *have* names in the Brothers Grimm version?

Fine. My name is... Blossom.

Settle down. Settle *right* down. It's a lot more manly in our language, believe you me. Anyone who wants to discuss the matter further, I'll be waiting, outside, afters.

Anyways. We seven are minding our own business, our business being the extraction of high-grade iron ore, when this giant does a breaking-and-entering on our mountain cabin. You could tell she wasn't the smartest cookie. You don't break into a miner's cabin and expect a warm welcome.

She spilled some sob story of an axe-wielding huntsman, but that's what happens when stepmothers with ambition become Queen. Simple heredity politics. Bit like a cuckoo. It's got *nothing* to do with beauty. 'Fairest of us all'? Pfft! Snow White didn't even have a beard.

36

We tried to warn her, really we did. We knew the old Queen wouldn't give up. But, after we'd trotted back to the rock face early next morning – and no, there was absolutely no Heigh-Ho-ing, not in an avalanche zone – what does Snow White do but let in the first thinly disguised pedlar who "happens" to wander by?

Finding a giant sprawled on your kitchen floor is enough to turn a beard gray, but we managed to save Snow White from a sorry end with a bit of bodice ripping and some mouth-to-mouth. I'm not at liberty to tell which of us...

Doc, you say? No, there was no Doc there. Yes, I'm *quite* sure. You done, boyo?

But, if it wasn't an over-tightened corset, it was a poisoned comb, and if it wasn't a poisoned comb, it was a rosy red, venom drenched apple.

That one stumped us. None of us thought to look down the damn fool girl's damn fool gullet.

It was sheer luck that some namby-pamby Prince offered to take her comatose body off our hands. Luck that the Prince manhandled Snow White so rudely that she up-chucked the slice of vilely poisoned apple.

Naturally, after a bit of cleaning up and rest assured, Princess vomit is just as foul as anyone else's, the two upper-class twits rushed away to get hitched. Bloody ingrates. We didn't even get an invite to the wedding.

Still, it wasn't a total bust. We People came out on top. We usually do, for all that we have further to climb. Who was it, do you think, that provided the high-grade iron for the old Queen's brand new pair of red-hot boots?

37

Tropical Surprise
by Irene Buckler

In its tall glass garnished with a pineapple wedge and strawberries, my Tropical Surprise looks delicious – and it lives up to its name. As the first sip slides down my throat, the surprises begin. Although she appears to be her bubbly self, I sense that Sally, who is sitting beside me, is seriously worried about something. I wonder why I have not noticed before. I suck up another mouthful of my drink and another, and before I can ask Sally what is wrong, I begin to experience an extraordinary awareness of how my other friends are feeling, too. Jane, sitting on my other side, is seething with hidden anger, while Robyn, who is sitting opposite, is full of secret anticipation.

After another gulp and without any extra effort on my part, I have an inkling that Sally has been sleeping with Jane's boyfriend, that Jane suspects as much and that Robyn is secretly meeting him later that night. Who would have thought?

I am exhilarated by my hyper-awareness, but the experience is still evolving and I am not so pleased when I get the feeling that my friends have not been forthright with me. Despite their assurances to the contrary, it seems to me that Sally, Jane and Robyn think I have been putting on weight. Eager to know whether Sally will tell me the truth about my expanding waistline, I lean towards her.

"Are you sure I am not getting fatter?" I ask.

I see that Sally's mouth is moving in reply, but whatever she is saying is drowned out by a rising cacophony of voices. Seeming to come out of nowhere, they are all inside my head, competing for my attention. I shut my eyes and cover my ears, but I am a conduit to every secret thought of every other patron in the crowded bar. Grasping at my glass, I gulp down what little remains of the Tropical Surprise. I need to get away.

Sally, Jane and Robyn are engrossed in conversation when I excuse myself from the table and head for the exit. As I step outside, I stumble, but to my relief, I am encircled and supported by my friends. Sally, Jane and Robyn have followed me.

"Her drink must have been spiked," I hear one of them say. "We'd better take her home."

As I am bundled into the taxi cab, a man from the bar approaches. He wants to share, but when my friends jump in beside me, his friendly face turns sour and I shudder.

"Another time," he hisses and is gone.

13 totara tottering
by Mercedes Webb-Pullman

In subalpine forests
totara is tallest.

If you don't shoot that possum I swear
I'll chop the bloody tree down myself.

Totara's top is really
a pantry.

Plump breasted pigeon,
possum pie perhaps.

as they chopped, chips fell amongst fleshy,
berry-like fruits littering the forest floor

Sleepless, kept awake by clickety-clack
as train on track passes over totara sleepers.

haven't you finished that carving yet?

Snow down to 600 meters, totara
tree tops white like meringue.

Totara is a strong sub-floor foundation.
Overhang is not a problem.

I have fenced myself with totara,
straight-grained and very resistant to rot.

(wave from the highlands to the montane)
Totara could survive in Scotland.

Totara's roots reach deep
to hold his head high.

Priming the Pump
by Elizabeth Bruce

One dollar? Is that enough? Who are you kidding, man? No way! One lousy dollar all by itself in a sax case? That's pathetic. Ain't nobody gonna get inspired by that. Shit. You ain't worth a damn dollar if that's all you got. You got to prime the pump, son, put at least five bucks there, plus a fist full of change. Quarters – make 'em quarters. None of this nickel shit. Damn nickels, ain't worth the time it takes a tall man to bend over and pick them up. You got to give folks something to *aspire to.* It's all about *aspiration*, son.

Go on, put some out there.

All right now – that's more like it. What's that? Six bucks and change? Good. Good. Wait a minute – these babies are damn near brand new. Shit, where you been, boy? This ain't the ATM. Crinkle them up. These babies got to look used, worn out, like they been living in wallets for years, stuffed down into pockets and shit, and you have *inspired* someone to take them out and give them *away.*

No, no, no, that's not it. Here – lemme show you. Turn some of them green side up, some green, some grey – make it look random, you know, like they just fell that way. All right, put some of them quarters on top, sprinkle them over there. Maybe a few dimes, make it look believable, you know.

Well, let's see – stand tall, y'all – how's it look? Yeah, that's better – a veritable bouquet of money just begging for company. OK, y'all ready? First train's coming in – you tuned up? No? Well, get on it, boy, hurry up. Come on now. Train's coming in. See the light? Your B flat's off, son, sharpen it up. Come on now: *do re me fa so la ti do...do...do..do... Do it! Good! Do ti la so fa me re do-o-o-o-o.*

Aspiration!

All right! It's show time, gentlemen, gimme one of Saint John's *Favorite Things*, which, God help us, never was, never will be, one of them lousy dollars. May Saint John forgive us.

Five, six, seven, eight....

For the Love of Chinos
by Jennifer Fliss

I was on the hunt for the perfect pair of chinos. Lately everything seemed too scratchy, too beige, too dad-like, too kid-like, too frat-boy-like. I wanted to wear them on a Saturday in the city. In the country, apple picking. For brunch... while eating an eggs Benny or just walking around with my hands in my pockets so I could shrug indifferently or coyly or smugly. I could be your chum or the source of your envy. I could turn the pockets out in a nod to Charlie Chaplin. I could keep my chino pockets a secret: only I knew of the bus pass, house key, and 43 cents. That's the glory of chinos; they can be everything. Sundays for the Lord. Weekdays for the man. I could dress them up with a sweater vest and didn't even have to wear a belt.

I once had a pair of magnificent chinos. 34L. I'm tall, need the longs. Color: twig. Bought on sale after Thanksgiving. Grizzly day, the clouds hung low and I was soaked to the knee. I wasn't wearing my beloved knee high argyle socks, so my calves were chilled. I now wear those delightful foot warmers daily. Now that I think about it, two revelations occurred that day. Like chinos, those socks have their place. But this is not the story of the myriad benefits of argyle.

So I had found the world's best chinos. I could toss them in the wash. Burrito droppings washed away like it had never happened. And then my ex-wife got them in the divorce. Claimed she didn't know where they were, but I knew. She couldn't bear their place in my life. In our lives.

44

She was a woman who bought me paisley socks for Christmas. I'll let that sink in for a minute: paisley.

I phoned the department store where I initially purchased the chinos. Nope. eBay – nothing. Goodwill. Craigslist. I couldn't find another pair of the pants anywhere. Did I make them up? Were they a figment of my business casual imagination?

I called the company and they told me they didn't carry that model anymore – the #951. In the economic downturn, they changed things up. They now outsourced to China, thus not guaranteeing the same level of conscientiousness that certainly went into the making of the lost chinos.

Are you interested in the #420? the woman on the line asked. Casual. Durable. Available in desert, mahogany, and Bordeaux. Bordeaux?! Blasphemy! A chino does not come in red. Thus it ceased to be a chino at all and was simply a slack. A pompous waspy slack.

In the meantime, I've been despondent. I can't wear just any pants. It is going to be a frigid winter. My legs are already cold. It's almost December and I am pants-less. I've gone on leave and am collecting disability. I sit in my briefs and, thank god, I still have my argyle socks.

Rear Window
by Susan Tally

It's not as if he mooned me:
Let me get over what never happened.
It's more like he let me watch
Through my window
As he took off his shirt in
Some parallel universe.
How many lovers did he remind me
of?
The distance between our buildings
Is filled with a few trees and patios,
But oh, was he in my space.
When he first moved in,
His creepy, climbing vine,
Then just a voodoo plant on a stool,
Made its showing in the window.
So odd, the plant held hallucinogenic
power.
I did not think about sunlight
Or how plants raised higher get more
of it.
And I never saw anyone inside.
That was before the woman appeared,
Acting as if they were in a play,
As if it were some big deal.

It was all about territory:
Where theirs began and mine ended.
Hovering, their muscles needed to be
sure that each would
Hold up their end of the curtain-rod
love-bargain.
They were so hot, hanging up their
long red window dressing
Which brings me round to why he
couldn't wear his shirt.

Riding the Mallory
by Neil Silberblatt

She says, her right hand timorously holding
her coffee cup, waiting for it to cool,
her left floating skyward like a Balinese
dancer, where it stops
five inches above her thick lustrous
hair, now tucked Lana Turner-like, though
she has no idea who that is.

She says that any prospective
lover must be at least this tall,
as there are certain heights
below which she will not stoop.

She says this as though she were
a barker at a carnival ride,
perhaps a tilt-a-whirl,
which the rider must be
at least this high to mount.

And I think of, and pity, those who
will have to wait to next year's fair to
ride the Mallory,
or satisfy themselves in the interim
with a less thrilling attraction.

The Height of the Door
by Robert Herron

Have you ever gone into a room and had to make sure
      that you didn't hit your head?
I've had to dodge under cabinet lights and
      particularly low ceilings
I was told that I should play basketball even though
      I'm terrible at it
I was told hockey isn't the game for me since I'd run the risk
      of injuring opposing players
I'm always looked at and asked "What do your parents
      feed you?"
It takes all my restraint to prevent myself
      from answering
"A nice, well-balanced diet that has nothing to do
      with my height"
I'm 5'10' at only 16 and I'm bound to keep growing
My dad's 5'6" and my mom's 5'2"
I don't want to be a basketball player or a freak
      in the Guinness Book of World Records
I just want to be me, a 5'10" guy who listens to metal,
      plays hockey and studies history
The only height that matters to me is the height I'll need
      to be to reach my dreams

Nature's Growth Potion
by Bear Jack Gebhardt

"You're so short," she said when she opened the door.

My heart sank. "I started smoking at a very young age."

We stared at each other. "You're Jeremy, right?"

"At your service."

"I'm sorry I said that. I was just ... surprised."

"If I'm too short, we don't need ..."

"No, no," she said. "Too short for ... well, anything real. Or personal, I mean anything permanent. Oh, what am I saying?"

I smiled, shrugged my shoulders.

"Sorry. You've probably already bought tickets ..."

I showed her tickets from my shirt pocket.

"I'm sorry. I shouldn't have ..."

And then she relaxed and smiled and my heart melted. She held out her hand. "Let's start over. Hi, I'm Rosalyn."

"Yes, I'm Jeremy. Quite pleased ..." Her hand was warm, soft and real.

"You were so smart and funny in your e-mails and on the phone. I was expecting ..."

"Someone taller?"

"Sorry," she said. "Let's forget I said that." She blushed. She was beautiful.

"The jury will disregard the counselor's statements and said statements will be stricken from the record."

Rosalyn looked confused, and then broke into a wide grin again. And again my heart melted.

"See," she said. "You're funny."

50

Funny is about the only arrow I have in my quiver. I'm five foot one inch tall, and my head is much too big and hairy for the scrawny body to which it is attached. Twenty years ago, when the Lincoln County Child Protection Services removed me from my stepmother's home – her prison – where I'd been kept in a basement room and fed twice a day, they reported that although I was thirteen I had the physical stature of a seven-year-old.

"I guess I should have warned you," I said, "Not about being funny, but about being ... well, being me."

"You *are* a strange-looking little man," she said. "Do you still smoke?"

"Smoke?"

"Yes. You said you started young."

"Oh, right. No, I don't smoke. Never did. That's just a line I use."

"Good," she said. "That would be a deal breaker."

"Wouldn't want to break the deal." I held the tickets up. "This deal, right? Still game?"

"Still game," she smiled. "I'll get my purse."

Four hours later, after the concert and dessert, we were back in front of her door.

"That was absolutely wonderful," she said. "I had a wonderful time."

"Wonderful," I agreed. Again she laughed. We'd laughed a lot. And then she was quiet and looked at me a long moment.

"I'd like to kiss you," she said.

"Wonderful," I replied.

"A goodnight kiss. To say thank you."

She slowly bent down, put her hand behind my head, kissed me softly, warmly on the lips.

"Thank you, sir," she said. "I want to think about this." She opened her door, stepped inside, turned, waved and closed the door.

That's how, walking home, I now measured six foot four.

Fiona's Miserable Serve
by Jenean McBrearty

For the hundredth time Arthur told Fiona Macy – yes, the daughter of Robert Macy, lawyer of tabloid fame – to plu-eez! keep the tennis balls inside the court. Arthur was a has-been Wimbledon competitor hired to improve Fiona's back-hand, not her track coach. But, following every lesson, he had to venture outside the chain-link enclosed court at the far south side of the Macy estate and retrieve her frighteningly powerful pop-up lobs from the woods that separated the estate from Lake Tahoe.

"It's the goddamned animal rights people," Robert told Arthur when he complained about sprinting through woods, and back. "God forbid a grebe or whatever *critter de jour* they're protecting get a ball in its gullet. I can afford the fine, but I say, if a damn bear is stupid enough to eat every yellow furry thing it sees, it deserves to die. It's Darwinian. Like Fiona's being six feet tall. But, what're you gonna do?"

Snap on the red-orange hunting vest over his polo shirt, hope PETA or the forest rangers didn't mistake him for a poacher or polluter, and round up every yellow furry round thing he saw within a half-mile of the lake. That's what he was gonna do. All the while cursing the measly five grand he'd make for scolding Fiona for three months, and convincing Robert her "potential" would eventually blossom into skill.

Today he couldn't find the third ball. Christ, could Fiona have hit it – snap! He saw his foot crushed between the teeth of a ground trap and realized he was in deep shit before he blacked out. When he came to, he was on the ground staring at a man in BDUs covered with leaves. Or was it just a tree wearing a wildflower hat and a grin? "You reckon this here's a Sasquatch?" another tree-man said.

"Call 911," Arthur pleaded.

One man squatted and said, "You're lucky vets found you before the smell of blood attracted the bear we're tracking." He pried open the trap and the other man pulled his leg away.

"Holy shit!" Arthur screamed.

"This trap ain't meant to kill. Just disable until we can get a knock-out dart in the bear."

"Now what?" Arthur panted.

"You'll lose that foot." One man took hold of him by the arm pits, the other by his knees, and carried him to a bunker they'd built between two trees. The vet gave him a tetanus shot, morphine, penicillin, and dressed the gashes in his foot. "Feel better?"

"Much. Call 911." The bunker walls were rife with rifles, bullet belts, and hand guns. Things looked dicey.

"Can't do that."

"You said you were a vet."

"I am. Iraq. A wanna-be hero who'll poach for any zoo for cash. Fucked up, but it's a living. Right?"

"No, it's opportunity." Arthur said. "You're really two campers who rescued me from the trap of a rich and negligent employer. Right?" The three exchanged knowing, approving glances. That's what Fiona gets for being so tall.

54

David & Goliath
by Guilie Castillo Oriard

Downstairs, the shouts and shrieks have turned into grunts and muffled cries. Daddy's in it for the long haul; Ma knows it, and is biting on something – a dishcloth, her arm – to avoid scaring the kids. But they are scared. They always are. Except this time they have a plan. And twelve-year-old Jacko, the oldest, the strongest, the one who's borne the brunt of Daddy's violence the longest, is the obvious choice.

Besides, he's the only one tall enough to reach the shotgun.

But he doesn't want to. He wants to put his hands over his ears, sit in a corner facing the wall.

"Whatcha waiting for?" Doreen, eight years old and looking like a baby in her pigtails, pokes a finger in his waist. But it's Emory, silent and wide-eyed, a year older than Doreen but the real baby nonetheless, who pushes him into action.

The barrel is awkward in his arms: too long, too heavy. He's used it before, hunting. Daddy insists his children – even Doreen – have to know guns, lose the fear, learn to kill. And he reserves special punishments for cowardice. The first time Jacko missed a shot, Daddy gave him a choice: twenty with the belt strap, or five with the buckle end. For years Jacko will wonder whether he chose the buckle as part of some sick, twisted logic to earn his father's respect, or because he knew that's what he'd get anyway.

The grunts continue downstairs, but the cries have stopped. The steady thump of flesh against flesh has turned wet.

"Go." Doreen pokes at him again.

The roaring in Jacko's ears masks the creak of the stairs as he descends. He needs to move fast, but each step feels like trudging through Jell-O. In slow motion he enters the kitchen, lifts the shotgun against his shoulder. He closes his mind to everything – the bloody bundle on the floor, the methodic rhythm of the kicks – and fixates on a spot just below the nape of his father's neck.

"Stop."

Daddy turns, also in slow motion. "Or what? You'll *shoot* me?" He seems genuinely amused. "Well, then. Whatcha waiting for?"

With his left shoulder, Jacko wipes sweat from his eyes. Then his chest heaves, and he realizes it's tears.

"You no-good pussy." Daddy's laughing now, coming closer. "Better pull that trigger, boy. Or I'll –"

Daddy's right; he is a coward. And now there'll be hell to pay. It's over in an instant. He's already lowering the shotgun when it's torn from his hands. Already cringing against that first blow, which never comes.

He watches, uncomprehending, as his Goliath slams backwards into the table and then, in a crash of shattered china and splintered wood, onto the floor.

But Jacko isn't David.

Emory is still holding the shotgun steady, saying – shouting? – something to Jacko, but Jacko hears nothing. The blast has left him deaf for real. He stares at Emory, half in terror, half in abject admiration, until finally the moving lips begin to make sense: *Is he dead. Is he dead.*

American Housewife
by Len Kuntz

It happened for whatever reason. Everything started to look different, distant, as if she was in an enormous cave, as if she was no more than a ragdoll dropped inside a gigantic mausoleum.

Her feet shrank first, then both femurs, each humerus, her clavicle and cranium. As her bones shortened, they made a cricking noise like concrete cracking.

No one seemed to notice.

Her sons, tall as redwoods now, fetched their own cereal, spilling milk all over the table as usual before leaving to catch the school bus. Her husband slurped his strong black coffee, reading the sports page while complaining about a referee's blown call.

She watched all this from her spot on the linoleum floor until the house was empty but for her.

Alone now, she continued shrinking to the size of a Pez dispenser.

Soon she'd be nothing, invisible, no different really, than when she'd been taller and normal-sized. She worried that her husband and sons would have to cook and clean for themselves. They'd have to iron and vacuum and dust, or else leave the house to ruin. Maybe they'd replace her with a taller version of herself.

But when Hemmingway, their calico cat, started circling her, fangs bared, she grabbed a stray toothpick off the floor, and charged. If this was it, she would go out swinging.

This is Barrow, But It's Not My Photo
by Kersten Christianson

I could be the tall gal
leaning over your shoulder,
taking in the 10 pm sunset view
through the wild fur ruff of your thick parka;
I've always had a thing for cold weather gear.

Or I could be the girl on a Honda,
revving across an icebound lagoon,
trekking along coast line
in the jagged shadow of pressure ridges.

This world is aglow in orange,
a frozen orangerie, like the one in Paris
only less famous, and older;
timeless like sea and ice.
There's no Monet here, no gilded water lilies;

only, the breath of Bowhead,
the whoosh of snowy owl wings,
the keen of wind,
scampering fox and giggling child.

This is Barrow, but it's not
my photo, and that is not you,
but it could be as I
inch closer to you, my steady windbreak.
This breath working that ruff,

while the light of the sun washes over us.

Confessions of a Remarkably Gigantic and Unbelievably Promiscuous Shapeshifter on Public Television
by J. J. Steinfeld

"I'm ashamed of my lifelong aberrant sexual behaviour in numerous shapes, with thousands of women and men since first realizing I've the ability to shapeshift, nearly 600 years ago," the remarkably gigantic, androgynous author, a fraction over eight feet tall, confessed directly into the TV camera, his head appearing to belong to an ordinary six-footer.

The skeptical TV interviewer, holding up the author's bestselling autobiography, with its provocative cover of a Hieronymus Bosch painting depicting a hellish existence, mockingly said, "Let's hope you write better than you confess," drawing laughter from the studio audience.

The remarkably colossal, androgynous author, shouted several words in an unfamiliar, mysterious language, and transmogrified into someone much smaller that no one recognized, Vlad the Impaler, and on public television demonstrated his most frightening and bloodthirsty shape.

Seeking
by Adina Sara

Tall…ish
Average build, a bit thicker in the middle but it all
    evens out
by the time I reach the ground.
Confident, not really, to be honest I've no idea
    why I keep doing this.
Prominent cheekbones I've been told (is that
    a good thing?)
and steady gait.

You would be lucky to nab me out of this
    list of 1,756 men
Aged 50-70
Seeking woman
Shortish, tallish, who cares
I don't even ask for svelte, happy to wrap my hands
    around a scrunch or two of fat
around your hungry edges.

Your age: unimportant. Except
you should be older than my oldest daughter
and younger than my last wife.
Also, the one before her.

Oh No.
I shouldn't have said that.
Can I delete?
Can I go back?
Maybe ten years
to a time when I was still tall…ish, a bit more confident,
limbs and loins more cooperative,
tastes more adventurous.

Oh the places I could have, would have, shown you
Oh the sloppy love I would have, could have
smothered you in.

I never cared if you were shortish, tallish, either way
I would have found your center like a bulls-eye.
I would have earned your grand prize.

How is it I'm still here, still seeking like
    there's no tomorrow,
hope shrinking along with body parts
Desire: A box left unchecked
Open mind: Check – well maybe, sometimes

Eyes, blue-green, behind dirty glasses
Stale bed-sheets
Fear of growing old alone
Check, check, check.

What else would you like to know about me?
Religion?
Income?
Favorite thing to do on a rainy Wednesday morning?

Just call me for God's sake. Or better yet,
come over. Bring a casserole, bring anything.
I eat anything.
Sit on my sofa, it's comfy, and tell me how fascinating
you would like me to be. I'll be it. At the very least
    I'll try.

Because there is no box to check that says:
Good Man.
I would never hurt you.
Try me. I won't bite.

Check.
Send.

A Redwood in the Yukon
by Wayne Scheer

Will Squires thought of himself as a man committed to words. But language betrayed him, like a lump of coal in a stocking cap. Although he loved the spark generated when words rubbed against one another, like two boy scouts in the woods, Will felt like a singer with a tin cup instead of an ear.

You see, language to Will was a slippery slope, a sloppy sloop, a silly slap, a salty soup. He just couldn't control himself; a circus performed in his head, all three rings, and he didn't know which to watch. His linguistic urges were as powerful as Superman's locomotive, able to leap tall buildings while bound to be little more than a bird baked in a pie.

He sat in front of his computer most every day trying to write simple, clear sentences. He admired Hemingway and Raymond Carver, but Tom Robbins inevitably slipped in a cowgirl with an enormous thumb or a talking fork. Like a chocolate bar melting in the hot sun, Will would lose his linguistic grip.

Language, to Will, caused as much confusion as finding his lover in bed with his wife. Still, he remained excited by the possibilities.

He tried writing a simple story about a man and a woman waking early one morning to an unknown sound. The plan was to have them search the house and, upon discovering nothing unusual, return to the comfort of each other's arms.

He decided to start his story with a simple sentence, but Simon's simplicity just wasn't in Will's house of cards. His red wheelbarrow overflowed with dancing bears left from when Ringling Brothers abandoned one of their rings.

He wrote:

"Morning dropped from the sky like a man parachuting from an airplane and landing on a field, not of dreams, but of pebbles that crunched as his boots landed with a thud and then skidded, sounding like a car on a dirt road."

He tried again:

"Ralph and Mary woke early in the morning, still mummywrapped in sleep, startled by a noise that may as well have been a spoken form of hieroglyphics because neither of them recognized the sounds, although between them they spoke seven languages."

Will studied his sentences, like a Comparative Literature major contemplating a '57 Chevy with the transmission spread out in pieces in his father's garage, asking, "What would Kafka do?"

That's when he experienced an epiphany. He was trying too hard to make sense. He saw reality as if he were looking through his own bifocals with one of the lenses set backwards and upside down.

So, like the first bicycle of spring, he accepted his vision and gave in to images of red-breasted Robin Givens. His commitment to writing remained as steadfast as a redwood in the Yukon; coherence, he decided, was as overrated as a porcupine without quills.

Poet Philosopher
by MK Punky

Let this be my manifesto
    to be tacked upon cathedrals and posted on digital walls
    where everyone in the world goes to look
    at what isn't happening to them.
It has thusly been decreed
    that He is I and I is She – another way to say
    that I is We, and She and You and all that ever was.
It's all in here.
Tall folks in the back, shorter in front. Everyone's invited.
Step right up.
It's all in here.

The decision has been made – by who or whom or what, no
one can say.
Royalty or slave, predator or prey, your divine purpose
is to be of service to God,
    God being Nature and living creatures and
    everything that's here and everything that isn't.
Your brothers and sisters, the ones who aren't born yet, the
ones whose shells
you might one lifetime inhabit – everyone is qualified.
Heretofore and hencewith, for seventeen millennia and the
next few hours,

I have myself convinced that the finest way to answer the
central question
is to share whatever it is one does best or most naturally or
with the most grace
and share it with the world
    really share, not merely as a flickering status update but how
the flower shares her pollen with the bee
    and he shares the fruit of his labor with us
    and we...
We write philosophical poems that aspire to be about
    something larger and longer than Eternity.

The Small Square
by Aaron Wiegert

Sticky note
On my door
Sings its lyric
Through yellow

I love you
In a pen
That's near
The end

I take it down
But I know
He'll know
I know, I

Stick it back
On the door
A bit lower
Though, as he
Is taller, he will

Take it down
As though
Nothing ever
Happened.

Skater Girl
by Robert Knapman

"What's ya name," she called over her shoulder as she rode off, throwing it out to the wind. She only half cared if he answered and even less if she heard. But that wasn't the point. The thing was she'd said it, and there it hung, her words, forming shapes, telling stories, building possibilities that bounced off the hot summer cement of the skate park where he'd been watching her.

He didn't call back. Instead, as if he watched himself, he let the words go carefully, clear in the afternoon sun. *"I'm Tom."* His name slid under the fluff of his young blonde moustache, lifting from his eager brown face and up over the scribbly gums. There it hitched on a gust and hurled even further, as if destiny was a thing, as if his name had a plan.

She slid to a stop. There was blood. The skin of her knee had opened but she'd hardly noticed till now. Earlier she'd skated too fast and lost control of the wheelslide. That was when she'd seen him, all legs, hair and eyes, before she crashed. She savoured that moment and stretched it out like she did when in the zone, when she felt she couldn't reach any higher. It was that moment when feet, board and air were a symphony of wild brumbies in a slow motion stampede and everything else seemed so small.

The thought evaporated and she noticed something as it fell towards her, its trail like the earth follows a drifting seed before it lands neatly and without fuss on willing soil. Cupped in her hands she peered at it as if it willed her to, as if the scratches and pain in her knees were all part of the plan. Then, after her fingers laid it out on the board's surface for a moment she slid it with care under the stained lip of her jeans pocket, committing it to her safekeeping, to the mystery of destiny and the seductive wonder of how it all comes to be.

Tall Fall Girl
by Neila Mezynski

Strewn over the far away floor in the round about white room, coat underfoot for the too tall loose footed girl. Tumble down down, hair flyin her length all over yellin for non skid shoes for a slippery ramp and a black coat on a white charger. Him. Tall enough.

Tryst with Emily
by Larry Lefkowitz

"No man, other than my father, has passed these stairs.
Nor here," she says, ushering me into her room.

"If not," I spar, "I would have soared to you
By this." I point to the window frame

Rope-raised basket she employs
To minimize human contact.

A deep belled laughter,
Unexpected, is my reward.

"You are interesting (she says,
Tall-seating me at a small table)

For your ... (serving me from a bone
China pourer) otherworldliness."

I fence: "Transported to your sphere
By poetic desire." I cannot resist

A glance past her pine-odored closeness
At the sturdy New England bed where I

Will remove her white dress
Worthy of a Poe heroine

To embrace the snowy presence
Underneath.

I rise to seize her
Standing so near on firm legs.

Then comes the knocking.
"That must be Mr. Whitman,"

She intones coolly, extending a
Farewell hand icy as eternity.

Another Objet D'Art
by Paul Beckman

Arthur hung around Calamities' Curiosity Shoppe for two hours trying to choose between the large dried hornet's nest and the glass sneaker with a cork in the laces. He knew Trudy would disapprove of either one and get on his case until he got rid of something else he collected. "The sneaker, I'll take the glass sneaker."

Once home Arthur took Windex and paper towels and soon the dust and dirt began to fall away. There was a heavy smudge and he put the sneaker down on the rug and took a dish towel to the smudge rubbing it back and forth. He loved how the sneaker looked like it was filled with spotlights.

Like a New Year's celebration the cork popped out followed by a black hand and a large black man who asked Arthur what the hell he was doing.

"Cleaning my new glass sneaker," said Arthur.

"Well, I'm in the middle of a playoff game and had to call a time out because you were summoning me. I've got thirty-six points and I don't have time for this."

"Are you a genie?"

"No. I'm a point guard."

"Aren't you a little tall to be a point guard? I'm six feet and you're at least a foot taller than me."

"I'm the smallest guy," Point Guard said.

"Now that you're out of the bottle what happens?" Arthur asked.

"I go back in and finish my game."

"What about my wishes?"

"Well if you want to see me again you'd better wish that my team wins."

"I wish that your team wins," Arthur said.

"That's one," Point Guard said.

"How many wishes do I get?" Arthur asked.

"As many as you want but I only grant a finite number that's figured by my performance. You should wish for me a triple double – that would be good for both of us."

Arthur wished for a triple double and Point Guard said, "That's Two."

"You'd better go," Arthur said. "Trudy will be coming home from her book club and you'll be hard to explain."

Point Guard dribbled a pretend ball around the sneaker and then dunked it in the hole and followed it.

Trudy rolled in after midnight smelling of wine not books.

"Arnold! Arnold!" Trudy yelled, waking him.

"What?"

"There's a giant basketball player lying on the couch. Do something."

"That's Point Guard, go to sleep or you'll wake him up."

Trudy passed out and Arthur woke early and made Point Guard some blueberry pancakes and they ate and talked and negotiated and finally fist bumped and Point Guard dove back into the sneaker.

Trudy came down in a great mood and saw the pancakes and told Arthur how thoughtful he was and she picked up the glass sneaker and said, "This is really beautiful, Arthur. Let's find the best spot to show it off after breakfast. I don't know how you do it," she said, "but you find the most interesting objets d'art."

75

Emergency
by Gwendolyn Joyce Mintz

Joanne had hoped her husband would be asleep, but he spoke as soon as she entered the bedroom.

"You were on there long enough."

"He wanted to talk."

"Stop babying him."

"I was listening and trying to help – that's what mothers do." She moved about in the dark, readying for bed.

Her husband grunted. "We don't have money."

Joanne slipped between the covers. "I said that."

"He said 'no'," she'd told their son when he'd called again about a loan. His baby was sick.

Joanne suggested he go to the emergency room. He could pay later.

"And more. Will you ask him again?"

"We have money."

"Not to loan."

"He didn't plan for a sick child weeks before payday."

"Should've had a kid when he could afford one."

"We didn't."

"No, we didn't. But did my father help us? Or yours?"

"You don't have to be like them." He had, in fact, sworn he wouldn't be.

"Well, they were right. Without their help, we learned to make it."

The receiver at her ear, Joanne wrapped the phone cord around herself as she turned this way and then that, away from her husband, him mouthing, 'We have our own bills.'

She listened to their son then faced her husband.

He set his face the way he did when he was determined not to be swayed by her tears. "Don't ask for money."

That would be a tall order, Joanne thought. She needed it now to buy a plane ticket to get to their granddaughter's wake.

Rwanda Suite: Slim
by Steven Gowin

Dawn after a late night gig. Slim had been looking for something.

On the high end of Rue des Martyrs he stopped for café au lait and watched October plane trees dropping big mapley leaves.

A month earlier, he'd packed his stuff for France. Paris was a better place for African Americans in those days. Josephine Baker sent a spray of roses; James Baldwin helped him find a good apartment.

From 1962 on, Slim gigged regularly, took minor roles in the movies – the wise American jazzman real deal jumpin' jive from Chicago, "Every Day I Get the Blues," and every day he became more and more Parisian.

Time to time the French Cultural Attaché toured him out as if to say, "lookie here America, you don't know how to treat folks; France do; we thumb our nose," of course forgetting Algiers and Dien Bien Phu.

In 1977 Slim played the Université Nationale du Rwanda on joint sponsorship from the French, his new home and the Americans, his old. He played stride style piano, played like a house afire, played with French pick up boys and Matt "Guitar" Murphy straight out of Chicago.

Afterwards, the Franco-Americans threw a reception at the Maison d'Accueil. Some of the English students, Jean Bosco, Honoré, Seraphina Anais, attended and certainly members of the Faculté Français (of which English was a part).

While the French congratulated themselves on superior culture, Slim sat on a low coach sipping whiskey straight. I parked beside him. I was one of the Peace Corps English professors. I appreciated his work, had seen a few blues men out of Chicago. Iowa City wasn't far.

I told him my girl had run away with another man and left me blue blue blue myself, and Slim said his gal had run off too but worse because he'd be damned if she didn't come back, true story. And he began laughing. I guessed I was a fool alright and laughed too.

About that time Seraphina Anais passed slowly, a tall shapely girl flashing a beautiful mysterious smile. Slim asked, what about these gals here, these African gals? Oh no, I told him, these were good Catholic girls, and you'd probably need to marry one to get far.

He looked down into his lap and thought a minute and finally looked up and asked what it would take, what a marrying would take? And I said I supposed you'd have to pay a bride's price, cattle.

Slim sipped his whiskey and glanced at Seraphina Anais and ran his free hand over that stripe of white hair on the front of his head.

Where you get them cows anyway?

coyote go see what's what
by Al McDermid

coyote he hungry powerful hungry
and they tall-walkers they movin' in
tearin' up the ground scarin' off
rabbit and snake they timid folk
don't like much coyote anyway
squirrel and mouse they stay
coyote still powerful hungry

yeah they tall-walkers they
movin' in buildin' they strange
hutches, they bright hutches
makin' rabbit get gone snake too
they bring some big others
some not so big others
some small others too

coyote but not puma but not
easier than rabbit sometimes
sometimes not
still tasty but too few

so coyote go down
down to the strange canyon
with the hard ground and
the big movin' run you down
you not careful yeah coyote
go down and see what's what
tall-walkers they dangerous
but they tall-walkers
they always have food

Tropes
by Mamta Dalal

Sandra looked up on hearing me enter her office. "Oh, it's you. About time. Sit," she waved towards the chair. Something about the papers in her hand was familiar. It was my manuscript!

"Vera, do you know who a millennial is?" My editor looked me in the eye as I settled into the chair.

"A what?" I echoed.

"Not what. Who. A millennial is, you know, someone born after the eighties or thereafter. A millennial is now our audience," Sandra stressed the last word. "You know, the late teens and twenty somethings…"

"That's right," I nodded my head. Rowena Publishers specialized in romantic fiction. Book sales statistics gave us our reader demographics. Though I hadn't been familiar with the term 'millennial'.

"Geez, have you been living under a rock, Vera? We are now catering to the millennial generation. They are into social networking, memes, and love online shopping. Our books cannot have these same old tropes anymore," she flipped through the manuscript until she came to the section she was looking for. "Robert was just the kind of man Cindy'd been dreaming about. Tall, dark, and handsome," she read out, then threw the pages on the table with a snort. "Tall, dark, and handsome, Vera, for God's sake! No one uses these tropes anymore. The world has moved on. Our stories need to be inclusive. You, on the other hand, seem to be stuck in the Barbara Coteland age!"

I didn't mind her caustic tone, I knew she meant well. "Cartland, not Coteland," I corrected her with a soft voice.

"Oh, whatever. But, you get my point, don't you? Your story is full of tropes. Sales are dipping like anything. This story is your last chance, Vera. I hope we can step up, if not we might as well shut down. Can you do it?"

She let out a sigh as if she was skeptical, even as she offered me a chance to redeem myself. Then she neatly placed my manuscript in her desk drawer and closed it with a single swift push.

I nodded. "We will. I'll revise it and submit it in a fortnight or two, I assure you."

I walked out with as much dignity as I could muster. Once I was out though, I was almost ready to break into a sob. Oh, dear, what was I going to do! At sixty-five, I couldn't go get any other job. As I neared my building, I bumped into O'Sullivan, the landlord. "Miss Skeet, the rent's overdue, ye know?"

"I'll pay it soon," I murmured and hurried into my flat.

Three weeks later, I was back in Sandra's office. She looked at me as though she'd never expected to see me return.

"Here," I handed her a thick manuscript. "I rewrote. Did away with most of the tropes. It has all new modern elements. The theme is very inclusive – it's a lesbian thriller romance," and here, my eyes gleamed: "And the protag is tall, dark, and handsome!"

83

Deception in Scarlet
by Tom Fegan

Sipping morning coffee at my dining table, I scanned the haunting news article. A profile of a tainted violent act in an upscale Dallas, Texas neighborhood five years earlier was splashed across the front page. Rachel Jones, a schoolteacher, was slaughtered in her kitchen. The attack occurred as her two-year-old daughter napped upstairs. Her husband Daryl, an engineer away on a business trip, had telephoned police requesting a wellness check. "She doesn't answer!" he'd pleaded. "I'm scared!"

I was Crime Scene Investigators' newest member. My throat tightened as I studied the scarlet-soaked corpse. A three-foot axe was found near the body, the door from the garage to the kitchen had been splintered, and a footprint and fingerprint were recovered. I began inquiries with neighbors and hit pay dirt next door to the scene.

A diminutive, bespectacled young woman opened the door. I displayed my badge, "I'm Mike Logan. May I ask you a few questions please?"

"I did it," Harriet Bates chimed. Stunned at her smugness, I arrested her.

The District Attorney's office confidently went to trial with a fingerprint, a murder weapon, the blood-drenched clothes she discarded before showering, plus a confession.

Harriet's statement included a brief affair with Daryl Jones. She and husband David, engineer for a competitor, socialized with their next door neighbors. Rachel confronted her about the affair and swung at her with an axe: "You can't have Daryl." A brief struggle ensued. Rachel was six foot and had the advantage but Harriet was short and wiry: she grabbed the axe from Rachel and killed her.

A tearstained Harriet Bates wept gallons and moaned self-defense under oath. She cried to the jury, "I fought for my life!" Harriet was a Cub Scout Den Mother for her two boys and a dedicated Sunday school teacher. Her error had tragic consequences. The jury returned a verdict of not guilty. Silent shock filled the courtroom. She had been implicated but not convicted.

Ninety days later Daryl Jones married his secretary. Harriet and her family returned to her home state of Georgia. She began a career as a licensed family counselor.

I folded the newspaper and picked up my Holy Bible laying on the table. I opened it and read Isaiah 43:8, "Lead out those who have eyes but are blind, who have ears but are deaf."

41 blows with an axe is not self-defense, it's murder.

I did my job, but who speaks for the sleeping child?

towering
by Kaytie Rose Thomas

Up on the tall hill that looks over the stadium in one direction and the ocean in the other, I remembered how we used to talk about Russia. I remembered the Moscow metro and your long opulent climb on the escalator to the surface, all that recycled air you told me about. You spoke Lenin's tomb into existence in my mind, and told me how your father had cracked jokes and grown tired of all the tourists. It's a beautiful city, you said. You love all its ugly history, and all its beautiful history, all its arching spires, stretching skyward. You are in the domes and you are in the spires, and you are tall like them, like the hill, towering.

I wanted to swallow your words, the sharp Russian phrases, jagged as coastlines, down past my teeth into my stomach, the center of me, then hold them inside – deep, deep down.

No Pink Elephants
by J P Lundstrom

When I woke up, he was watching me. His eyes closed slowly, the longest lashes I had ever seen, and when they opened again he smiled. At least, I think he did – I wasn't sure.

"You're a giraffe."

He answered reproachfully. "You shouldn't make fun, just because someone's tall."

"I'm sorry – I didn't mean to hurt your feelings."

"Don't worry about it." He peered at me between the branches. "How do you feel?"

I thought about that. "I have a doozy of a headache."

"I had a hell of a time getting you home." He was amused. His long, sinuous tongue surrounded a leaf and it disappeared into his mouth.

"Where am I?"

"I brought you to my acacia." He wiggled his tongue and batted his eyelashes. "You had a little trouble getting up here."

I assessed my situation. My arms were draped around a pair of the acacia's limbs; my legs clung intimately to its trunk. "How long have I been here?"

"Not long." He moved closer, until we were eye to eye. "Stay as long as you like."

"Thanks very much for looking after me," I tried my best to be polite. "But I really think I'd better be getting home."

"Well, then," I watched his long neck as he swallowed, then turned away. "Watch out for ants on your way down!"

"What? Ouch!" I felt a paralyzing sting, and the acacia, swayed by gravity's more convincing claim, released my arms and legs. Then Eek! my left hand grabbed a clump of thorns, Oof! My shoulder banged into a branch, and Ow! My right knee whacked the trunk. On my way down, I vowed never to take another drink. I landed hard on the ground.

When I woke up, a koala was holding my hand.

The Resting Chair
by Michael Koenig

the work is quite violent/
she stands/ receiving
food/making the next
one/go/ all the way/
through/ she goes through
you/ and draws metallic/
you/ you can lick it off/
you/ and
taste her/ past/ you/ find it
funny/ you/ do not laugh/
her cheeks are parallel/
and/ stretched as
canvas/on wood/ taut for
squinting/ she trips/ over a
joke/ does not laugh/
does/ not find it funny/
darkness/ does/ help her
bloom/ her feet round/ as
eggs/ the spiral takes a
minute/ then settles/ at the
base/ wrestling with
safety/ her own/ she can't
contain/ the pressing/
can't lay/ flat like a cover/
and soak in the resting
chair/ her wick is moist.

Bruce Almighty
by Mark Hudson

Bruce is tall. I'd say six foot something. As a grown man
and father, his body has filled out. But in my adult
      art class, we
were talking about what misfits we were in
      high school. (Which
is why we find refuge in an art class as adults.) Bruce said
freshman year in high school he was the tallest kid in high
school. He went out for the basketball team, and after three
weeks on the team, he was kicked off for scoring a point
for the wrong team. For some reason, this made me feel
I could relate to him more.
On Saturday my friend Chris joined the class late,
and I had set up my art station, and went to the Seven Eleven
to get a Big Gulp. It was gigantic, and I spilled a bunch of it
trying to find the correct size lid. I finally settled
      for a slurpee
lid and brought it to class.
When I brought it to class, everybody was shocked at
the "Tall" drink I brought. Tall Bruce said something to the
effect of, "It needs wheels!" And I said, "Sort of like the
Black Sabbath song, 'Lost in the wheels of confusion',"
and Chris said, "No, more like the Black Sabbath song,
'Fairies wear boots'."
The class is a portraiture class, and the instructor

told Bruce to focus on the hand as a subject matter. Somehow, it brought him down memory lane to a seventies Chicago television horror show called 'Creature Features' in which there was an episode called the 'Gunslinger's Hand', that had a possessed hand that was going around, creeping around, possessed.

At the end of the class, the Tall Big Gulp must've worked as a diuretic, and I left nature's artistic creation in the tiny restroom toilet of the studio. Bruce said, "Well, this painting might as well go into the toilet," and I said, "Maybe there could be a hand coming out of the toilet," and on that note, we knew it was just another "tall" tale.

Double Tall
by Cameron Filas

"Rum and coke. Double. Tall." Geoffrey leaned against the bar top, rolling up his black sleeves.

"That'll be eight bucks." The bartender set the drink in front of Geoffrey, who dropped a ten on the counter. "Anything for your lady friend?"

Geoffrey shook his head and took a sip from his drink before walking back to his table.

"They were out of cranberry juice," Geoffrey said, taking a seat next to a short brunette in a red dress.

"Really? What kind of bar doesn't carry cranberry juice?" Melinda turned to glare at the bartender.

"Apparently, this one."

"Well, I don't want to just sit in a bar with no drink. Let's go back to the room." She pulled a small mirror from her purse and began redrawing her lipstick.

"When I'm done." Geoffrey took another sip.

"Geoffrey, come on. It's freezing down here."

"They don't like when people bring bar glasses up to their rooms."

"Who said that? I've never heard that." Melinda dropped her mirror and lipstick back into her purse and snapped it shut.

"Why don't you go up and take a shower? I'll be back up there before you're out."

"I'm not going to shower if we're just going to you-know-what when you finally come up. Then I'd have to shower again before leaving."

"Well, if you're cold you should head up and turn on the thermostat." He swirled his drink slowly, watching the dark liquid whirlpool in the tall glass.

"You know I don't like fiddling with those things."

"Fine. You want to go back to the room now? Let's go back."

"Okay. But what about your drink?"

"I'll just bring it up." Geoffrey stood up from his chair.

"I wouldn't want you to get in trouble. Sit down. I'm feeling a bit hungry now anyways." Melinda waved to a hotel waiter near the bar.

Geoffrey rubbed his stubbly face and let out a sigh. "Why do you do this?"

"I don't know what you're talking about, dear."

"See? You just did it. That's what I'm talking about."

"Did what, Geoffrey?"

"I'm here to get away from the petty bullshit in marriage." Still standing, Geoffrey took a long draw from his drink. "And it's like I have two wives now."

A waiter, clad in a white oxford shirt and grey vest strode to the couple with a notebook in hand. "Would you like to place an order, ma'am?"

Melinda held up a thin finger to the waiter and turned to look at Geoffrey. "Just because I want to chat and eat a meal together before we screw does not make me some overbearing prude."

"It's casual sex, Melinda. Casual! I don't want to play husband when that's exactly what I have to do at home!"

The waiter stepped back, clutching his notepad to his chest.

"Fine." Melinda stood up, snatched her purse, and marched away. Her red dress floated about her hips as she pushed through the doors.

"Uh..." the waiter said.

"Just," Geoffrey sighed. "Another rum and coke. Double. Tall."

Awakening
Her Choicest Powers
by Jan Elman Stout

He believes she is his wisp of a woman, legs slender as silk thread, feathered raven hair spilling and swaying as he directs her. He names her back's curves, memorizes her breasts' singing ripples, and duets with her a cappella, thick fingertips plugging his own ears.

The folds of his fingers tumble over his gold band, the pale twinkle of a rapidly dying star. Head back, chins undulating, stomach churning, he snores, sloshing like the sea. His eyes pop open and greedily he drinks of hers.

He tugs and pulls and yanks but cannot rise. He pawns his dread and she welcomes it, swallows it whole. If she gulps enough he will disappear. She pulls his cupped hands from his ears and croons. Her diamond flickers, concealing her promise to her sisters.

And his sylvan sleep returns.

She pivots away, tall legs never parting. Like him, she is seduced by molten slumber. In dreams she floats in the Tyrrhenian Sea and kisses Capri's craggy coast, lapping its reefs with her teasing tongue. She climbs aboard his approaching ship while her sisters' lure serenades. Straddling him, unlashing his petulant girth from the mast, the sea beneath is calm as glass.

It waits.

The Giant's Height and Mine
by Glen Armstrong

It's only natural to long

for creatures who can see
a little further down the road:

Nephilim, Lovelock Skeletons,
50 Foot Women wondering
how they'll ever be loved.

Lincoln's enormous marble lap

(should D.C. security
momentarily lapse,)

would have to be checked at sunrise.
They would find the lot of us
huddled together.

I would swing on the blue–
skinned Asura's
wheel of arms.

My friend the Yeti
would boost me onto his shoulders
to better see the parade.

I would run to keep up
with my giant's stride.

He would let no harm befall me.

Tony Robbins Told Fred to Follow Others' Dreams Instead of His Own Because They Thought Bigger

by David S. Atkinson

They say to dress for the job you want rather than the one you have, but I don't know if I've had much luck growing my height to six-foot-four and putting on too-small dark suits. The addition of platform shoes may have helped a bit, but I think putting an "Angus Scrimm residence" sign out front was overboard... even if I did move to a small town mortuary first.

For some reason, people thought I was a theatrical basketball player. I guess they all equate "tall" with only one thing and anyone not affiliated with the sport can go lump it. I found myself under contract as a villain fighting the teamup of the Harlem Globetrotters and Scooby Doo, despite my inability to even dribble.

I didn't get discouraged though. I built an army of flying chrome spheres that could shoot drills and blades out their fronts, filled them with brains from corpses I then shrunk down into little trolls. No real idea why, but that's what I did. Unfortunately, the trolls kept getting confused with the Sand People from Tatooine. Next thing I knew, I was doing voice-overs for a Lawrence of Arabia-themed Star Wars amusement park and leaving flaming bags of ocelot excrement on George Lucas' front porch.

It wasn't quite the career path I'd been hoping for.

I imagined the metal balls would have kept things straight more, but they apparently gave the impression I was trying to stump for a pinball machine version of the whole scheme. The Federal Reserve simply explained that arcades weren't too profitable these days, but promised to keep my idea in mind in case the business landscape changed.

Perhaps I should have been speaking up more. Repeating "you play a good game, boy" certainly wasn't enough. In fact, I think it reinforced the pinball mistake. Listening to Elton John tunes didn't help my case either.

Of course, eventually they were all part of my army anyway, their husks turned into trolls and their brains floating in my balls. Whole lot of people died as part of that, let me tell you. Maybe I didn't think that part through, though their mistakes didn't make much of a difference at that point. After all, no one was left alive to employ me... but I did have my less than enviable armies. Still, though I came close with my plan, I'm still just not quite who I set out to be.

Try as I might, I'm still only a tall-ish man.

My Bed is Getting Taller
by Tim Philippart

An exit strategy for
Getting out of bed,
Was not needed.

I just dis-embedded,
Every morning,
For years.

Now one foot paws,
Afraid of what it will find,
Cautious as a toe in an alligator pit.

Each night the bed gets taller.
Will my legs and feet,
Handle the fall?

Each morning a leap of faith,
I hurl myself off the bed,
Maybe two inches.

I get older,
The bed gets taller,
The floor might disappear.

There is Nothing Worse
by A.J. Huffman

than finding a bathroom
obviously designed by a short person
when you are tall and your knees end
up at your ears after you fall
for what seems like forever, ass
slapping against frigid porcelain. I always feel
like a child being punished for being
able to reach the top shelf. I want
to scream at the vertically challenged
architect, force understanding down his throat.
Cower has never been an appropriate position for relief
of bladder, but if it must be endured,
then there should at least be support bars for assistance
and leverage when it is time to get up.

Collectors and Immigrants
by Sean Jackson

She didn't even ring him first, she just used her key and walked right in with a pair of movers who stood the canvas in the middle of the living room and then left.

"Oh Jesus," he said, coming in, not yet dressed. "That's way too big."

Micha said no, it was totally fine.

"Tall is coming back," she said. "Tall is chic again."

"No, that's way too tall to put anywhere," he said. He said it was like a banner that hangs from a downtown art museum. "I'm not hanging any banners in here," he said.

"Evan," she said. "Evan," she repeated, then tossed her hands. She stood beside the canvas, roughly the height of a basketball goal (only an arm's length wide), and stared into the corner of the room. Glass walls met at the crease, which made that spot problematic. Same thing with the other corner.

"What about there?" she said, pointing to the center of the east wall, which housed a floor-to-ceiling width of sheetrock painted tombstone gray. She said the photographs hanging there – three, stacked vertically – would have to go.

"That's my grandmother," he said, wrapping a throw around his shoulders because the day outside was cold and sunless. He stood beside her and held a mug of coffee. "And my adorable grandfather."

Micha bit her lip, crossed her arms, and then shook her head.

"They are forever destined to be immigrants," she said. "Another move isn't going to kill them."

He glanced at her. She had the expression of a woman who was prepared to push the red button, the one with the nuclear codes.

"Well, I'm not doing it alone," he said, sipping his coffee. "Where'd your guys go?"

She said the movers went downstairs to finish another job. Two jobs, same building, a company that knows how to streamline efficiency.

"Did they paint that picture?" said Evan, lowering himself into a big chair, a chair that could hold a giant. "They sound so talented, did they make it on the way over?"

She sighed. Sometimes the collectors are worse than the artists. Nowadays, most of the time. There is no polish to anyone anymore. She explained that this artist had died of blood cancer just recently. An older woman. She died alone, in a crappy apartment, with – it's been said – a volume of poetry under her mattress that once belonged to Kafka.

"So dreadful," Evan said. He felt Micha was playing the guilt card. *Just shut up and hang the painting*, she was saying. He waved her into a chair while they waited for the movers to come back and become hangers.

"That's so terrible for a person to die like that," Evan said, watching the clouds scuttle down the river, sometimes above the smaller buildings, other times seeming to drift right through the taller ones.

Micha nodded, leaving her chin high.

"Almost as bad as living like that," she said.

Standing Tall
by Ruth Sabath Rosenthal

I bequeath myself to the dirt to grow from the grass I love,
If you want me again, look for me under your boot-soles.
Walt Whitman, *Leaves of Grass, Song of Myself*

Walt, it's over a century since you bequeathed us
your long, fluent lines so filled with optimism
and exuberant trains of thought on laborers and lovers,
trees growing tall in your youth. Trees that now
        stand sky-high
in airs rank with intolerance, limbs reaching upward
entreating heaven. And I quake in the timbre

of unrest that surely would have waked you
in a drench of sweat – waves of foreboding darkening
optimism a far cry from

leaves you'd garnered upon the greenest grass;
a far cry from the blush of autumnal hues winter's cue
that snowflakes dance upon bare branches

reaching far and wide, warming wanting hearts,
enlivening the earth with a melt giving way
to burgeoning spring on earth. Earth, where today,

flags raised, nation after nation, wave
shamelessly. O Walt, if only you were here
to unearth the green of grass now scorched

in these flagrantly hostile days.
If only you were here to help raise hope
with your inimitable ebullient praise of green.

Jenga
by James Croal Jackson

Stack the words three by three,
two by three, one by two
        by one
when you try to know a person
because you always pick
the lover who never stays bound
            to one,
the ones who twist the shape
    and stability
        out of their bones
        piece by piece.
Build a life together.
    Structure and release.
Remove what makes us stand.
Clouds never reach their hands
            too far
        before the collapse,
        truths sprawled on tile.
When it happens,
                we won't
            have the will
        to pick our pieces
                off the floor.

106

Spirit Week
by Martha Rand

"It's not fair! It's not Fair! It's NOT FAIR!"

It was early in the morning and the school social worker was listening to the frequent refrain of her eleven-year-old counselee.

"You're right, sweetie. There's a lot about life that's not fair."

"You don't understand, I have all the short players on my team!!!" the young girl stamped her feet. "It's not FAIR!"

There was no point in interrupting too soon. The young girl would have to wear herself out a little before she could hear the school social worker's response. Besides, it was true, most of the 6th graders were not as tall as the 7th and 8th graders. And, in Spirit Week, the tournaments were grade against grade.

"When life isn't fair, sweetie, we all have to reach inside ourselves and find the best way to respond. That's how we develop inner strength and the ability to do our best in the face of what we're dealt."

The young girl leaned forward, in the comfy red chair across from the desk, arms wrapped around her stomach, and bared her teeth.

"You're a good player. I've watched you at recess. When you play basketball, I can see that you're thinking. You're strategizing how to make the shots."

The eleven-year-old gazed up to make eye contact with the social worker. Her mouth softened and she shook her head as she whistled out a breath.

"Go out there today. Play your best game. Be a great player. Maybe, you can even be a generous player and make the rest of your team look good. That's what a great player does. They play their best game and they make the rest of their team look good at the same time." The social worker paused. "I think you can do that."

The young girl stood up, still angry. She left the room to return to class.

The tournament took place that day during the long recess that combined lunch and gym time. The 6th grade came in second. The 7th grade came in first. The 8th graders and the faculty team came in third and fourth.

During end-of-day homeroom, the social worker and the young girl sat in the same chairs they had sat in earlier that day.

"Your team did a good job. You came in second. You guys worked well together. What do you have to say for yourself, now?"

The eleven-year-old thought hard. "Maybe I should have had more faith in my friends?"

"This morning you accepted that you weren't going to get your way. You played your best. You demonstrated good teamwork, and," the social worker paused, "you're willing to reconsider your behavior. Good job, today."

Oil & Cheese / Chalk & Water
by Winston Plowes

His golden hair was flyaway,
her straightened locks jet-black.
For him the combing over,
for her the scraping back.

In the attic he lived upstairs,
below him she lived down.
Crude oil on her still waters,
their private tinsel town.

He walks amongst the skyscrapers,
she's down with bungalows.
He bangs his head on doorways,
whilst she looks up his nose.

A solitary big fish was he,
amongst sardines she's fine.
He's a lonely only child,
and she was one of nine.

the tall brunette
by Robert Beveridge

love is easy
easy as pie
easy as walking
down the corridor
of the Franklin Mills Mall,
that own-the-world walk,
eyeing girls
in low-cut blouses
   short ruffled skirts
and loose jackets,
trying to catch
a fleeting glimpse of one
evasive breast,
one oscillating thigh
beneath ruffled denim.
Easy as reaching
out to caress
the hair of a stranger,
knowing she'll never
see you again,
but needing that touch
all the same
It's the kiss that's hard—
telling the tall

brunette behind
the fast-food counter
that she's beautiful
is easy—leaning
over and pressing
hungry lips against hers
isn't

Red Shoes
by Michael Webb

Andrea could never shake the feeling that she was getting dressed to please everyone else. "Find your style, what makes you feel good, what works for you," all the magazines said, but as long as she could remember, looking in the mirror confronted the universe of other people's opinions. First the slavering glance of boys, then the cold predatory gaze of men, and always in the background, the constant chorus of disapproval from other women, her mother foremost among them.

"You can't pull that off," Mom would say as Andrea came down the stairs as a teen. Her skirt was too short, her blouse too loose, her ungainly height making her too tall for girls' sizes and too slim for women's. It was a constant struggle, but Andrea was never one to confront authority, stomping back up the stairs to find something to suit all the invisible rules that hemmed her in. She would not back down, but she would not defy either.

"Momma?" Andrea's daughter Amanda said. Amanda was 4, all snarled hair and willful obstinacy. She had, after much discussion and tears, been allowed to begin selecting her own clothes. Today, she was wearing blue and white striped tights, a purple skirt, and a green top, all shades that clashed hideously. Andrea tried not to laugh.

"I wanna –" Amanda began.

"Honey," Andrea interrupted. "Are you sure you want to wear those tights? They are –"

112

"My favorite!" Amanda said, her tiny jaw setting. She could see her husband Kurt in Amanda's face. That's all you, hun, Andrea thought. All you.

"Of course they are," Andrea said. One of her favorite parenting blogs said, "you have to decide what hill you want to die on," and her daughter looking like she had dressed in the dark wasn't a fight she was prepared to have.

"Momma, I wanna ponytail," Amanda said.

"What's the magic word?" Andrea said automatically.

"Ponytail, please," Amanda insisted, and Andrea followed her back to her room.

When Andrea returned, she looked at her reflection again. She tugged her dark skirt into place, the firm taut triangle that fell just to her knee, and tucked her ivory blouse in a tiny bit tighter. She stepped forward and into her shoes. They were red leather, very expensive, and as high as she dared, much higher than her mother would have allowed. Andrea felt the power in being taller. She relished the way she could command a room with her assertive stride, making her words punch like a boxer and slice like a razor. She was ready for them, ready to overcome their objections, ready to answer questions and assuage fears, and ready to make this deal happen.

Andrea was ready, and she left her bedroom for the last time that morning, her shoes tapping out the rhythm of her heart.

The Deal Breaker
by Alex Robertson

Categories to complete
Boxes to tick
In filling out the website form
On an internet dating site

"A writer (poet)
        and social activist
From a country town
Seeks soul mate
Into folk music and science fiction
ABC viewers only need apply…"

Once past the questions
Clicking and scrolling through it all
Exhibit A has a cute smile
        full and flowing hair
But only 5' 3"
Less than adequate
For an oversized dark mysterious type
Continuing his search in vain
No Amazonian types to be found

Later in his quest
Matches are presented via email
Daily selections fulfilling his criteria
Attractive in various ways
Physical splendour and sapiosexuals
However
          mostly vertically challenged

Matches found
Some loftier than the average woman
But no giantesses by any means
Issues recognized besides
          a lack of chemistry
Incompatible star signs and interests
Nothing that links their stories together

He searches for the one
Ticking the majority of boxes
Thinking it will never happen
Holding out for hope
Even if she is tallish…

Memory Palace
by Gary Percesepe

after James Tate

The house was dark and solitary. I walked around back and tried the door. It was locked. Black rotted vines covered the crumbling brick walls of the house. The vines pulled off in my hand, useless for climbing. The moon peaked out from behind a cloud, illuminating a fire escape. I climbed to the landing on the top floor where I encountered a tall man named Steve. He was just leaving, he said, but I was welcome to join him. "What's inside?" I asked. "It's a memory palace," Steve said. "What's that?" I asked. "You're here for Jennifer," he said, "aren't you?" "How did you know?" I asked. "Everyone comes by here looking for her," he said. This seemed implausible. I knew several people, maybe dozens of people, who didn't know Jennifer. I told Steve this. "Nonsense," he said, "Jennifer lives in the Memory Palace, we've been waiting for you." We entered the big living room together. The room was littered with old records, 45s and 8 tracks and CDs, comic books, baseball cards. A pile of fringed cowboy clothes rested on a winged backed chair, all sizes. Batons and whistles, cheerleader uniforms with matching underwear, sports bras, boots and shoes, tie-dyed T-shirts, and loads of costume jewelry. There were children's books and coloring books and brightly colored sticker books and glitter makeup, but everything seemed to belong to the same childhood. The bath toys looked lonely on the living room floor, holding

116

traces of the children from whom they'd departed. I felt Jennifer's familiar gaze coming from a painting on the wall but when I mentioned this to Steve he laughed. "Look again," he said. I looked and there were no paintings on any of the walls. "What you feel looking at you is from the Jennifer you brought here. You're responsible. In the Memory Palace nothing is ever lost, everything is just misplaced." I went to the window and looked down at the ruined French garden. An old man in a police uniform was there to arrest me. "But officer," I said, "I'm an old man." "And yet this is your first visit," he said. Steve brought us cups of tea served from Jennifer's silver tea service. We sat in the garden drinking. Jennifer waved from the wide window.

In Freedom and Love
by Daniel de Cullá

There's nothing more to know
Than what I am
When I found the other side of what I want to be:
Europe is a Prison of refugees and migrants¡
Through its windows, we are seeing mountains
Reservations, rain and clouds over
The Valley of Freedom and Love
Faced on a daily basis of slight
A highway overgrown with seed
And hands that yearn for eyes
A camp where we have been stopped
Hearing sounds ears to Earth
Inside the ground
Flashing the light through the wood
Over the stream expecting to see the end
On the same line of our dreams
Living with dignity
Free from fear, persecution and oppression
Where we are like a wheel
Cracking air on air, spinal membranes
Already feeling our bodies down bags
Ready to start for a new place
Suddenly realizing our freedom
Coupled with the conscious plane
Of being Homo sapiens
Not Christian and fundamentalist
Cannibals.

The Stature of Motherhood
by Cynthia Leslie-Bole

I used to be tall, I swear it. At least tall...ish.

Plenty of women were shorter than I was. I was told the average height for a woman in the US was five feet two inches and I was five four. I found it reassuring to know that I held my head at least somewhat high.

When I became a mother, I towered over my tots as they wrapped their arms around my thighs, and for a time all was well with our relative proportions. Every year they set growth goals, excitedly wondering when they would reach my belly button, then my shoulder, then my chin, then actually – dare they hope? – my same height, the height of a bona fide grownup.

Well, we should have pulled the plug right there on the growing business, but my two formerly tiny toddlers insisted on using their burgeoning cells to unfair advantage, and they continued to add an inch or more a year to their height.

First my daughter shot past me, until I had to look up to make eye contact with the newly statuesque girl. Somehow I didn't feel like I was providing the proper mothering experience when I had to stand on tiptoes to smooch her or reach my arms upward to hug her.

It just didn't feel right, but at least my son still showed proper maternal respect by staying well below my chin for many years. That is, until he didn't. Maybe it was all those spinach and protein smoothies I made him choke down during high school. I should have given him something less nutritious because before I knew it, he was suddenly towering over me with a self-satisfied chuckle. There's nothing worse than the smug grin of a newly tall child draping his arm around you and saying, "Hello, little mama!" What temerity.

So now for the first time I actually feel short. I may have lost a smidgen of height as I've aged due to spinal compression, but this situation really isn't my fault. It's their fault, those who cheekily shot upward in pursuit of sun and sky like giant sequoias, leaving me standing way down here in the mulch of terra firma. In my own eyes, I have somehow become a short woman, a ground-hugger, kin to earthworms and stink bugs and dung beetles (who really aren't such bad companions after all).

I do my best to act like a real mother from below, but it's hard to muster the appropriate gravitas when you feel physically like a child in relation to your own children.

"But Mama," they say with their voices full of comfort, "good things come in short packages."

They say it tenderly, then they kiss me on the top of my little head way, way down here.

The Skyscraper
by Ben Pitts

Your copy of *To Kill a Mockingbird*
    dog-eared page 352:
"He was carrying Jem. Jem's arm was dangling
    crazily in front of him."
It took the work of four paramedics
to lift you on the gurney. Your arms
were so long, they skimmed the gym's
hardwood floors on your way out.
Nothing could be done when your hands
suffocated any hope of driving to the rim.
But I never did make it to your games.
You sat in the back of my class, knees
trapped outside of the desk. "Can you see?"
I asked too many times. You never moved up.
You circled chapter 31,
"I found it incredible that he had been
    sitting behind me all this time."

Passage
by Tom Sheehan

I can't recall when I am tall,
the after-effects of alcohol,
so I will try when I'm to die
not to go with my throat gone dry;
just pour some gin in my coffin
so I can fly what I fly off in.

Hawaii
by Todd McKie

My wife used to drive me nuts.

Sweetheart, she'd say, Don't smoke inside, the cats have asthma, remember? Ralphie, please stand up straight. You used to be so tall, now you're all stooped over. I wish you'd drink your beer from a glass, Honeybun, this isn't a trailer park.

One day when Donna was bugging me I flipped out. I told her I was going to get in my car and drive west, all the way to Hawaii, drinking beer and smoking three packs a day. And slouching whenever and wherever I pleased.

News flash, Ralphie – you can't drive to Hawaii, Hawaii is in the middle of the Pacific Ocean.

I know where Hawaii is, I said. When I get to California I'll sell the car, buy a boat and sail to Hawaii.

Brilliant plan, she said, But you don't know how to sail and you get seasick. Remember that whale watch? A certain someone stayed below and projectile-vomited while everyone else was on deck experiencing, up close and personal, the biggest mammals on the planet shooting water out of their blowholes. You missed the whole thing.

Those waves were huge. And I wasn't the only person who got sick.

That gal was a disabled senior citizen and she got sick because you stunk up the entire boat, Captain Ahab.

I grabbed a beer from the fridge, lit a Marlboro right in her face and banged out the door. Last thing I heard was

123

Donna hollering, Drop me a postcard! and laughing like a mental patient.

The Toyota quit outside Wheeling, West Virginia. I sold it for peanuts and took a bus to L.A. where I worried that gangster rappers would knock me out and steal my pants. I asked the first American-looking person I saw where could I buy a sailboat. Marina del Rey, the geezer said. One a them sailor boys'll sell you a boat faster'n you can fart.

The sailboat thing didn't work out, because even the small ones were pricey. Also, I realized a giant wave could swamp the boat and wash away my provisions and I'd have to catch fish with a shoelace and eat them raw and drink my own urine. I hate sushi. I flew to Honolulu on an airplane.

I'm on a beach in Hawaii. It's part of the USA, but Hawaii's like a whole different country, an exotic, tropical one with Asian-type individuals everywhere and pineapples practically jumping into your mouth. Palm trees are swaying all over the place, and they're beautiful, but watch out for falling coconuts unless you want to get knocked out cold as a cucumber.

I'm dancing barefoot in the sand. The sand is hot and I'm doing the hula. It's an updated version of a traditional hula because I'm smoking a cigarette and drinking beer from a can while I dance. Those are my own personal touches. Don Ho, eat your heart out!

Medium
by Lara Lillibridge

I am medium. Brown hair, brown eyes, medium height, weight, and shoe-size. My brother is tall, and by tall I mean outside the bell curve. He says he's six-foot-nine, but my mother thinks he's closer to six-foot-seven. All I know is that if I stretch my hand as high as it can go, I can just reach the top of his head. Like telling a fish story, when someone asks how tall my brother is, I just say, "he's this big."

My sister is short. At four-foot-nine, she is legally a dwarf. People tell me that a legal dwarf isn't a real thing, but if you google 'dwarf', they have height maximums. Maybe 'legal' isn't the right word, but I need something to explain that I am not exaggerating.

My siblings have rendered me height-blind: if you aren't as tall as my brother or as short as my sister, you are just "people-sized." This has led to a lot of arguments with friends who insist they are tall or short, when clearly they are within normal distribution. It may also explain why my three LTRs were with men who are five-foot-seven, the same height I am. You're either people-sized, or you're not.

My brother wasn't always tall – I mean, he was tall-ish, but not the tallest kid in class. He just refused to stop growing. He grew well into his twenties. I always think it was somehow intentional – he outgrew his bullies, he grew so big our parents couldn't ignore him, he grew until people started looking at him as the one in charge. And my sister wasn't always short. She just stopped growing one day when her thyroid went on strike and she never fulfilled the potential her foot and hand sizes promised. It was like she just decided not to be a bother and just stopped requiring larger-sized clothing. Me? I was always just medium, but I also didn't want to stand out. I spent all of high school trying to be Just Like Everyone Else, so maybe my height was also intentional.

My medium-ness is actually height privilege. Neither my brother nor my sister can help standing out. I always have the option to blend in, to hide out in the back row, to just be another nameless, faceless, fortyish mom-type. I can always find jeans in the proper length. I never hit my head on ceiling fans and I don't need a booster seat when I drive. No one IDs me when I buy alcohol and no one asks me, "how's the weather up there?"

It was only recently that I decided that average wasn't something worth aspiring to. When I realized that maybe blending into the crowd wasn't some higher calling, I had to work a little harder. Stand up a little straighter. Color my hair and learn to be funny. Maybe if I hadn't been given the option of being just like everyone else, I would have chosen a more interesting existence.

Purple Shorty
by Shayla Hawkins

You know the crazy thing? Purple wasn't even his favorite color! He told me that once, but he never said what his favorite color was. He was like that: told you just enough to get you interested, then dropped the convo and never mentioned it again. But one thing he did every time he saw me was call me by my nickname, and I returned the favor. For the ten years I worked for him, it was the running joke between us.

"Yo, Shorty," he said one time before a concert, strutting out of his dressing room in a canary yellow pantsuit and matching platforms. "You ready?"

"I stay ready, Purple Shorty," I said. I checked my earpiece and patted the pistol inside my blazer.

He spun around, still walking. "You keep calling me 'Purple Shorty,' and I'm gonna knock that grin off your face," he said, grinning himself.

"You have to reach my face first, Purple Shorty, and that'll be hard, especially if you ain't wearing your little boots."

He laughed and turned back towards the stage. His hands were made for stroking women and guitars, not for fighting; and next to my solid 7-foot-1-inch frame, his 5-foot-2 self looked like a little pony. We were David and Goliath, and I think he liked that, because it reminded him that even though I was the giant with the brute strength, he was the one with all the favor and glory.

I can't say one bad thing about working as his bodyguard. Because of him, I saw the world, made good money, and had fine women rubbing up on me because they wanted to get close to him. (I never let it happen.) And the music? Man, it didn't get any better. His Superbowl halftime show in Miami, when the sky opened and seemed to pour down at his command during 'Purple Rain'? I was there, never forgetting I was his guardian first, and then a fan, but fully aware of the genius I was watching.

The only thing that could make me leave that job was getting married, which I swore would never happen. But it did, and it was my wife who called me that Thursday morning.

"Are you driving?" she asked.

"Yeah. Why?"

"Pull over," she said.

I did. Her voice broke. "He's dead, Reynaldo."

I couldn't think or move for 20 minutes after that. When I did, I turned my Jeep around and drove to Paisley Park. I walked past satellite trucks and TV cameras to the perimeter fence, where people were leaving purple flowers and balloons. I looked up, and towering over my head was the biggest rainbow I'd ever seen. I threw up my hands.

"All right, Purple Shorty," I laughed. "You got me."

I couldn't explain it, but I knew that was his way of flaunting how he was finally taller than me, and that, though he was gone from this world now, he was enjoying every minute of his cosmic ride.

Authors

Alex Reece Abbott

writes across genres, forms and hemispheres. Published here and there, Alex's literary historical novel *The Helpmeet* was a 2016 Greenbean Irish Novel Fair winner. Her contemporary novel, *Last of the Lucky Country*, shortlisted for the 2015 Northern Crime Competition. A Northern Crime Competition and Arvon Prize winner, her short fiction often shortlists, including for the Sunday Business Post/Penguin Short Story Prize, and Bridport Prize. She barely blogs at www.alexreeceabbott.info.

Glen Armstrong

holds an MFA in English from the University of Massachusetts, Amherst and teaches writing at Oakland University in Rochester, Michigan. He edits a poetry journal called *Cruel Garters* and has three recent chapbooks: *Set List* (Bitchin Kitsch), *In Stone* and *The Most Awkward Silence of All* (both Cruel Garters Press). His work has appeared in *Conduit, Otoliths* and *Queen Mob's Teahouse*.

David S. Atkinson

is the author of *Not Quite so Stories*, *The Garden of Good and Evil Pancakes* (2015 National Indie Excellence Awards finalist in humor), and *Bones Buried in the Dirt* (2014 Next Generation Indie Book Awards finalist, First Novel <80k). His writing appears in *Bartleby Snopes*, *Grey Sparrow Journal*, *Atticus Review*, and others. His writing website is http://davidsatkinsonwriting.com/ and he spends his non-literary time as a patent attorney.

Paul Beckman

was one of the winners in the Queen's Ferry 2016 Best of the Small Fictions. His 200+ stories are widely published in print and online in the following magazines amongst others: *Connecticut Review, Raleigh Review, Litro, Playboy, Pank, Blue Fifth Review, Flash Frontier, Matter Press, Pure Slush, Metazen, Boston Literary Magazine, Thrice Fiction* and *Literary Orphans*. His latest collection, *Peek*, weighed in at 65 stories and 120 pages. Find his website at: www.paulbeckmanstories.com.

Robert Beveridge

makes noise at xterminal.bandcamp.com and writes poetry just outside Cleveland, OH. Recent appearances include *Chiron Review, Riverrun*, and *Third Wednesday*, among others.

Elizabeth Bruce

is a DC-based writer/theatre artist originally from Texas. Her debut novel, *And Silent Left the Place*, won Washington Writers' Publishing House Award, with distinctions from Texas Institute of Letters & *ForeWord Magazine*. She has been published in *Gargoyle, FireWords Quarterly, Inklette, Bare Back Magazine, Lines & Stars, Gravity Dancers, Long Short Story, Washington Post* and you can find more about her at her website here: http://washingtonwriters.org/wordpress/portfolio-item/elizabeth-bruce/

Irene Buckler

is a person who loves making things and teaching others how to make them. She has written and illustrated many stories and poems, educational activities and programs – some of which have been published by others in hard copy and online, and some of which have published on her website *Mrs B's Interactive Literacy*. Find it here: http://members.ozemail.com.au/~irenelesley/public_html

Guilie Castillo Oriard

is a Mexican writer and dog rescuer living in Curaçao. She misses Mexican food and Mexican *amabilidad*, but the island's diversity and the laissez-faire attitude (and the beaches) are fair exchange. Her work has appeared online and in print. Her first book, *The Miracle of Small Things*, was published in August 2015 by Truth Serum Press. She blogs at http://guilie-castillo-oriard.blogspot.com and at http://lifeindogs.blogspot.com/.

Kersten Christianson

is a raven-watching, moon-gazing, high school English-teaching Alaskan. Currently she is pursuing her MFA in Creative Writing/Poetry through the University of Alaska Anchorage and will earn her degree in July 2016. Her recent work has appeared in *Cirque, Tidal Echoes, The Fredericksburg Literary & Art Review, We'Moon* and *Heartbeat: A Literary Journal*. Kersten co-edits the quarterly journal, *Alaska Women Speak*. She lives in Sitka, Alaska.

Martin Christmas

has an M.A. in Australian Cultural Studies and is an Adelaide-based performance poet, photographer, and professional theatre director. He was a Friendly Street Poets mentored poet in 2012 and has been published in several anthologies. He teaches poetry presentation elements to young spoken word poets. In 2016 he will curate Adelaide photographer Adam Durst's one-man photographic and poetry exhibition.

Samuel Cole

lives in Woodbury, MN, where he finds work in special event management. He is a poet, flash fiction geek, and essayist enthusiast. His work has appeared in many literary journals. He is also a prize-winning scrapbooker.

Megan Crosbie

is a queer writer who lives in Scotland with her partner. She spends most of her free time writing very short fractured fairy-tales and other works of flash-fiction. Her writing has been published around the world, both online and in print. When not writing she enjoys urban exploring, drag shows, and too much wine.

Mamta Dalal

works in the technology industry by the day. She writes now and then and also loves cinema and travel. Her stories and features have appeared in various publications including *StoryHouse*, *India Currents*, *HuffingtonPost*, and *National Geographic Traveler India*, among others. Two of her works were also part of international anthologies. She is based in Mumbai, India.

Daniel de Cullá

is a writer, poet, and photographer. A member of the Spanish Writers Association, Earthly Writers International Caucus, Poets of the World, he is also the Director of *Gallo Tricolor Review*, and *Robespierre Review*. He has participated in Festivals of Poetry, and Theater in Madrid,

Burgos, Berlin, Minden, Hannover and Genève, and has exhibited in many galleries from Madrid, Burgos, London, and Amsterdam.

William Doreski

lives in Peterborough, New Hampshire, and teaches at Keene State College. His most recent book of poetry is *The Suburbs of Atlantis* (2013). He has published three critical studies, including *Robert Lowell's Shifting Colors*. His essays, poetry, fiction, and reviews have appeared in many journals.

Kristina England

resides in Worcester, Massachusetts. Her writing has been published in several magazines, including *Gargoyle*, *Muddy River Poetry Review*, *New Verse News*, and *Silver Birch Press*. Her first set of published photos appeared at *Foliate Oak Literary Magazine* in April 2016.

Tom Fegan

was raised in his family's downtown Fort Worth Restaurant Burger & Shake. After college he spent several years in the steel industry and is presently contentedly divorced and works as a security professional. This gives him opportunity to pursue his writing career.

Cameron Filas

writes short, flash, and micro-fiction. His work is published at *Yellow Mama*, *Shotgun Honey*, *Jitter Press*, *365 tomorrows*, *Nailpolish Stories*, and *Five 2 One Magazine*, among others. He lives in sun-baked Mesa, Arizona, with his fiancée. Read his other stories and follow his blog at cameronfilas.com.

Jennifer Fliss

is a Seattle-based fiction and essay writer. Her work has appeared in *The Washington Post, Narratively, Prairie Schooner, The Citron Review, Necessary Fiction,* and elsewhere. When not writing, she can be found with her kid and / or cat, running, reading, and on the flying trapeze. Seriously. Follow her *@JFlissCreative* and learn more on her website, www.jenniferflisscreative.com.

Bear Jack Gebhardt

is an old guy living in the foothills of Colorado, USA, with his patient wife of a hundred years. Two of his most recent books are *The Potless Pot High: How to Get High, Clear and Spunky without Weed,* and *The Smoker's Prayer: Spiritual Healing of Tobacco Addiction with or without Chantix, Nicotine Patches, Hypnosis, Jail Time or Duct Tape.* You can find also one of his websites here: TheSmokersFreedomSchool.com.

Steven Gowin

is a corporate video producer in San Francisco. His fiction has appeared in *The Santa Fe Literary Review, In Case We Die, Insomnia and Obsession, Olentangy Review,* and others. Gowin is a graduate of the Iowa Writers' Workshop. He blogs here: http://thebayviewsg.wordpress.com.

Shayla Hawkins

is a poet, fiction writer and Detroit, Michigan native whose writings have appeared in, among other publications, *The Caribbean Writer, Windsor Review,* and *tongues of the ocean.* She has also been a Prince fan since she was four years old and wants readers to know that Prince's small physical stature while he lived is inversely proportional to the massive, eternal impact his music has had on her heart.

Robert Herron

is a student from New York. He thinks of poetry as a wave that could be ridden if you make sure that you're prepared to surf in it. He himself is tall compared to his family at 5'8 and has been asked about his height.

Liam Hogan

is a London-based writer. He hosts the award-winning monthly literary event, *Liars' League*. Winner of Quantum Shorts 2015 and twice finalist in Sci-Fest LA's Roswell Award, he has been published at *DailyScienceFiction* and in *Sci-Phi Journal*. You can find more of his work at http://happyendingnotguaranteed.blogspot.co.uk/.

Mark Hudson

is a poet, writer and artist who has contributed works worldwide. This is his second contribution to a Pure Slush book, and he also has a poem up on their website. He had to submit to tallish twice to come up with the right poem, which is good news to all of you would-be-writers who are frustrated. Keep submitting!

A.J. Huffman

has had poetry, fiction, haiku, and photography appear in hundreds of national and international journals, including *Labletter*, *The James Dickey Review*, and *Offerta Speciale*, in which her work appeared in both English and Italian translation. She is also the founding editor of Kind of a Hurricane Press: www.kindofahurricanepress.com.

James Croal Jackson

is a US-based writer, composer, and occasional filmmaker originally from Akron, Ohio. He rediscovered his love for poetry during time spent in Los Angeles. His work has been recently published in *Whale Road Review, Euphemism, Rust+Moth,* and other journals. He currently lives in Columbus, Ohio. Visit him at jimjakk.com.

Sean Jackson

has published numerous short stories in literary journals from the U.S. to Canada and Australia. In 2011 he was a Million Writers Award nominee. His debut novel *Haw* was published in 2015. He was born in Raleigh, North Carolina. He lives in Cary with his wife and two sons.

Robert Knapman

is originally from Sydney and has been described as a visual poet who intuitively sees emotion. Robert discovered writing in his 20's to help process his travel experiences. Recently his poems were featured on a number of Sydney bus shelters. His *Jonny and Dave* street art project (Sydney 2010-2013) was featured in *Verity La* and shows how Robert combines words and his love of visual images. His FB poetry page is https://www.facebook.com/SweetDarkScent/.

Michael Koenig

is an emerging queer poet and creative writing major at the University of Adelaide. His work is mainly concerned with queer anxieties, the beauty of nature and housewives (real or otherwise). When he's not writing poetry he enjoys overanalyzing PJ Harvey records, vegan food, avoiding social media and gardening.

Len Kuntz

is a writer from Washington State. He is an editor at the online magazine *Literary Orphans,* and the author of *I'm Not Supposed to be Here and Neither Are You,* out now from Unknown Press. You can find more of his work at lenkuntz.blogspot.com.

Larry Lefkowitz

writes stories, poetry and humor and has been widely published in journals, anthologies, and online. His humorous fantasy collection, *Laughing into the Fourth Dimension* is available from Amazon books. His humorous literary novel, *The Novel, Kunzman, the Novel!* is available as an eBook and in print from Lulu.com and other distributors.

Cynthia Leslie-Bole

is a writing coach and editor and has been published in the online journal *Rootstalk* and *Moonshine Ink Creative Brew*. She lives in the San Francisco Bay Area with her best friend/husband and is the mother of two amazing young adults. Her first collection of poetry, *The Luminous In-Between*, was published in March 2016. Find her website at www.cynthialesliebole.com.

Lara Lillibridge

is a recent graduate of West Virginia Wesleyan College's MFA program in Creative Nonfiction. In March of 2016 she was a top 5 finalist for DisQuiet's literary prize in Creative Nonfiction, judged by Phillip Graham. She has had essays published in *Polychrome Ink*, *The Feminist Wire*, *Airplane Reading*, *Thirteen Ways to Tell a Story*, and *Weirderary Literary Magazine*. Some of her work can be found on her website www.LaraLillibridge.com.

J P Lundstrom

grew up and attended college in southern California. Her writing most often is set in that warm, often dangerous place known as Los Angeles during the mid-twentieth century.

Current books are *Adventures of a Young Girl* and *The Fruit of the Poisonous Tree*, both available on Kindle. She strives for easy reading, not that intellectual stuff; she doesn't like to waste time on deep thoughts.

Jenean McBrearty

graduated from San Diego State University, and taught Political Science and Sociology. Her fiction, poetry, and photographs have been published in over 150 print and on-line venues. She won the Eastern Kentucky University English Department Award for Graduate Non-fiction (2011) and a Silver Pen Award (2015) for her story *Red's Not your Color*. Her serials *Raphael Redcloak: Guardian of the Arts*, and *Retrolands* can be found on Jukepop.com.

Al McDermid

writes speculative (i.e. genre) fiction, magic realism, and occasionally Brauniganesque poetry. He is also the author of *All That Is*, a collection of poetry based on the Chinese classic, the Tao Te Ching, and is the co-author (with Aki Liao) of two throwback, hard-boiled mysteries set in post-WWII, pre-statehood Hawaii. His literary role models are Henry Miller, Richard Brautigan, and Robert E. Howard (and if that combination makes sense to anyone, please explain it to him).

Jolene McIlwain

teaches literary theory / criticism part-time at Chatham and Duquesne Universities in Pittsburgh, Pennsylvania. Her fiction has been twice nominated (as Honorable Mention and Top 25 Finalist) in *Glimmer Train*'s Very Short Fiction contests. Her work appears in *The Fourth River* and *Five Pure Slush Vol. 10* and is forthcoming in *Prairie Schooner*'s Sports Shorts series. This is her chocolate Lab, Hank's, first appearance in a published story. You can tweet her at @jolene_mcilwain.

Todd McKie

is an artist and writer, staggering from canvas to keyboard, bleary-eyed and paint-spattered. His stories have appeared in *PANK*, *McSweeney's Internet Tendency*, *STORY* (online), *Chicago Literati*, *Litro*, and elsewhere. Todd lives in Boston and blogs sporadically at toddmckie.blogspot.com.

Neila Mezynski

is a dancer turned choreographer, abstract painter, found object "sculptor", installation artist and writer of chapbooks, eBooks and pamphlets.

Gwendolyn Joyce Mintz

is a writer and photographer working from the deserts of New Mexico. She has authored two chapbooks, *Mother Love* (Unlikely2.0) and *Where I'll Be If I'm Not There* (Argus House Press). Find more of Gwendolyn's work at her blog here: http://wwwonewriter.blogspot.com.

Gary Percesepe

is Associate Editor at *New World Writing* (formerly *Mississippi Review*) and a Contributor at *The Nervous Breakdown*. He is the author of seven books, including *itch*, a collection of flash fiction, and *falling*, a poetry collection, both published by Pure Slush Press. Percesepe teaches at Fordham University in the Bronx. He lives in White Plains, New York.

Tim Philippart

sold his business, retired to explore, to write and discovered he wasn't very retired at all. He ghost blogs, writes poetry, non-fiction and an occasional magazine piece. He loves writing and wishes he had not waited decades to pick up the pen. He sees baseball as a metaphor for... Oh, he's sorry, he keeps promising not to do that. Send emails to timphilippart@yahoo.com and visit www.imaginiscent.net.

Ben Pitts

is from Phoenix, Arizona. A High School English teacher by day and a renegade poet by night, he lives with his wife, Brianne and daughter, Grace. His poetry has been featured on several websites and journals and most recently in *The Machinery* literary collection.

Winston Plowes

lives aboard his floating home in Calderdale with his lucky black cat, Fatty. He teaches creative writing and was Poet in Residence for The Hebden Bridge Arts Festival 2012-14. His collection of surrealist poetry *Telephones, Love Hearts & Jellyfish* (Electric Press) was published in northern spring 2016. Find his website at www.winstonplowes.co.uk.

MK Punky

is the best-selling author of many books. His essays, articles and poems have appeared everywhere from small literary journals to the *New York Times*. MK Punky's poetry has won several international writing prizes, most recently the 2016 Stratford-upon-Avon Literary Festival's Creative Writing Contest, celebrating Shakespeare's 400th.

Melisa Quigley

is a writer and poet who came second in the 2015 City of Glen Eira My Brother Jack Awards for her short story, *The House on the Hill* and commended for her poem, *Ice Cream*. You can find other examples of her work at her website here: melisaquigley.wordpress.com.

Stephen V. Ramey

lives in beautiful New Castle, Pennsylvania, with his wife and two reformed feral cats. His work has appeared in many places, including *The Journal of Compressed Creative Arts*, *The Doctor T. J. Eckleburg Review*, and *Every Day Fiction*. His collection of (very) short fictions, *Glass Animals* (Pure Slush Books), is available wherever fine books are e-sold. More at www.stephenvramey.com and on facebook and twitter (@svramey).

Martha Rand

is a writer and artist. Her fiction has been published in Pure Slush anthologies *obit*, and *barcode* as well as at the Pure Slush online site. Her work has been read at galleries in New Jersey and at KGB in New York City. Her artwork has been shown in juried shows in New York and New Jersey. Ms. Rand has been a Licensed Clinical Social Worker for over 20 years. ArtsHealer.com is her website.

Alex Robertson

was born in Adelaide and has spent his early working life around (country) South Australia and the Northern Territory. He has been occasionally published, first in university student publications and then in journals. Since his location to outer Adelaide, he has tried his hand at short stories for his own interest. He is also involved in writing groups in Gawler and the North East suburbs of Adelaide.

Ruth Sabath Rosenthal

is a New York poet, well-published in literary journals and poetry anthologies throughout the U.S. and internationally. In October 2006, her poem *on yet another birthday* was nominated for a Pushcart prize by *Ibbetson Street Magazine*. Ruth has authored five books of poetry: *Facing Home* (a chapbook); *Facing Home and beyond; little, but by no means small; Food: Nature vs Nurture;* and *Gone, but Not Easily Forgotten*. Purchase these books from amazon.com, or ruthspoems@aol.com. For more about Ruth, visit her website at www.newyorkcitypoet.com.

Adina Sara

currently divides her time between pulling weeds and writing. Oakland-based, her novel, *Blind Shady Bend,* tells of an elderly woman whose life takes a sharp, unexpected turn. Her memoir, *100 Words Per Minute,* offers a look into the heart of clerical workers. In *The Imperfect Garden,* she explores the elements of determination, disappointment and surprise that shaped both her landscape and life. Visit her at www.adinasara.com.

Wayne Scheer

has been nominated for four Pushcart Prizes and a Best of the Net. He's published numerous stories, poems and essays in print and online, including *Revealing Moments* (https://issuu.com/pearnoir/docs/revealing_moments), a collection of flash stories. His short story, *Zen and the Art of House Painting,* has been made into a short film: https://vimeo.com/18491827. Wayne lives with his wife in the U.S.

Martin Shaw

has been writing for around ten years. Born in Luton, Bedfordshire, he grew up in the city and escaped to the Lincolnshire fens before moving to Cleethorpes. He writes in the mornings and late evenings, loves his family and thanks you for reading his work.

Tom Sheehan

has had 24 books published, been nominated for National Book and Military Book Awards, has 30 Pushcart nominations, won short story awards from *Nazar Look* for 2012–2015 and had multiple work in *Rosebud*, *Linnet's Wings*, *Serving House Journal*, *Copperfield Review*, *Literary Orphans*, *Indiana Voices Journal*, *Frontier Tales*, *Western Online Magazine*, *Provo Canyon Review*, *Nazar Look*, *Eastlit*, *Rope & Wire Magazine*, *The Literary Yard*, *Green Silk Journal*, and others.

Neil Silberblatt

has published two poetry collections: *So Far, So Good* (2012), and *Present Tense* (2013). He has been nominated for a Pushcart Prize, and received Honorable Mention in the 2nd Annual OuterMost Poetry Contest (2014). He is also the founder of Voices of Poetry, which has presented poetry events, featuring distinguished poets and writers, at various venues throughout CT, NYC and Cape Cod, and he is the host of the Poets Corner program on WOMR/WFMR (out of Provincetown, MA), for which he has interviewed acclaimed poets both on and off Cape Cod.

Rita A. Simmonds

received her BA from Hofstra University and her MA from Teachers College, Columbia University. She is a three-time winner of the Best Original Poetry category at the annual

Catholic Press Association Awards. In 2012, fourteen of her poems were featured in the bestselling *MAGNIFICAT Year of Faith Companion,* and 49 original poems in *MAGNIFICAT Year of Mercy Companion.* In 2013, she published her first book of poems, *Souls and the City.*

D.M. Simone

identifies – in a world where everyone seems to be looking for an adequate label to stand out and yet fit in – as transatlantic European. Based in Berlin, she's a writer / producer / journalist with a degree in American Studies and English. Her mind works in four different languages, but she is also fluent in pop culture, food, and 20th century vintage.

J. J. Steinfeld

lives on Prince Edward Island, where he is patiently waiting for Godot's arrival and a phone call from Kafka. While waiting, he has published sixteen books, including *Disturbing Identities* (Stories, Ekstasis Editions), *Would You Hide Me?* (Stories, Gaspereau Press), *Misshapenness* (Poetry, Ekstasis Editions), *Identity Dreams and Memory Sounds* (Poetry, Ekstasis Editions), and *Madhouses in Heaven, Castles in Hell* (Stories, Ekstasis Editions).

Nancy Stohlman

is the creator and curator of the Fbomb Flash Fiction Reading Series in Denver, and her work has been nominated for a Pushcart Prize. Her books include *The Vixen Scream and other Bible Stories, The Monster Opera, Searching for Suzi: a flash novel,* and four anthologies including *Fast Forward: The Mix Tape,* a finalist for a 2011 Colorado Book Award. You can find out more about her work at www.nancystohlman.com.

Jan Elman Stout

is a native Chicagoan who lives with her husband in Washington, D.C. Her work is published in *Pure Slush*, *Literary Orphans* and the *Journal of Compressed Creative Arts*. Jan is an Assistant Fiction Editor at *Indianola Review*.

Susan Tally

works in New York's Public School 163 as a literacy tutor. One of her favorite subjects to write about is her cat Zoey. Her poems have appeared in *Birds Piled Loosely* (Issues One and Five), *Clementine Poetry Journal* (Volume 1), *Kind of Hurricane Press* (Anthology 3, 4).

Kaytie Rose Thomas

is a writer of sorts from Southern California, who now resides in the lovely grey city of Aberdeen, Scotland. When not writing, she can be found wearing yellow sweaters, and crying about Haruki Murakami. Her poetry has been previously featured in *The West Wind*, *Whale Road Review*, and *Rust + Moth*. You can follow her at twitter.com/neptunesongs.

James Wade

lives in Austin, Texas, where he writes fiction for his wife and two dogs. His wife is encouraging, but the dogs remain unimpressed. He is the Winner of the 2016 Writers' League of Texas Manuscript Contest for Historical Fiction. His work has appeared in *Jersey Devil Press*, *Skylark Review*, *Bartleby Snopes*, *After the Pause*, *Potluck Magazine*, *Typehouse Magazine*, and others. Visit his website at www.jameswadewriter.com.

Alan Walowitz

has been published in various places on the web and off. He's proud to be a Contributing Editor at *Verse-Virtual*, an Online Community Journal of Poetry, and is also happily employed as a teacher of teachers at Manhattanville College in Purchase, NY and St. John's University in his native borough of Queens, NY. Alan's chapbook, *Exactly Like Love*, was published by Osedax Press in 2016.

Michael Webb

wonders about life, the universe, and everything in suburban Philadelphia, Pennsylvania. His writing can be found at michaelwebb.us.

Mercedes Webb-Pullman

gained an MA in Creative Writing from Victoria University, Wellington, in 2011. Her poems and short stories have appeared online and in print, including *Turbine, 4th Floor, Swamp, Reconfigurations, The Electronic Bridge, Otoliths, Connotations, The Red Room, Typewriter,* and *Cliterature,* and in her books. She lives on the Kapiti Coast, New Zealand.

Aaron Wiegert

has penned two chapbooks, *Evil Queen* (2013) and *The Last Railroad Spike* (2016), both from Budget Press. He is also Poetry Editor at *Drunk Monkeys* webzine. Aaron's works have appeared in literary journals and anthologies throughout the U.S. as well as Australia, Canada, England, Scotland, Austria, and Nigeria. Send him an email at aarondwiegert@gmail.com.

Other books from Pure Slush

Visit the Pure Slush Store:
http://pureslush.webs.com/store.htm

Feast!
ISBN: 978-1-925101-62-1

Five
ISBN: 978-1-925101-71-3

Rattle of Want
ISBN: 978-1-925101-67-6

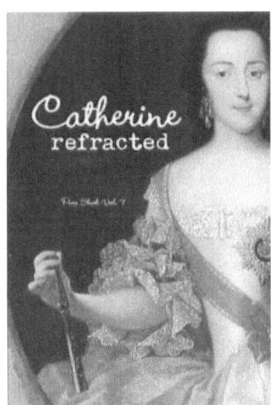

Catherine refracted
ISBN: 978-1-925101-78-2

The Vixen Scream
ISBN: 978-1-925101-11-9

Many Fish to Fry
ISBN: 978-1-925101-59-1